The

Lighted

Eugénie Giasson

Published by Hemingway Publishers

Cover design by Hemingway Publishers

ISBN: Printed in the United States

Dedication

To Mike, the man who made everything possible.

Acknowledgment

I want to thank Jennifer Gehlhar, Carson Davies, and Jayne Reyes for correcting my grammar and for making the book easier to read. Thank you to Paramount for helping me to self-publish my book. Thank you for your patience.

Sincerely,

Eugenie

Contents

Chapter 1
The Beginning

All stories have a beginning. This one started in a ceramic studio in Cape Cod. The studio was absolutely cluttered with all styles of pots, plates, statues, really anything that could be made of clay. There was a large kiln in the corner, shelves and shelves of paints, clay, and finished and unfinished projects. Abel Smith and his wife, Clara, had lived in the same house since they got married. She looked a bit like him, in the way that people who are married for a long time tend to look. There was no order to the place, but Abel knew where everything was. He was an old man, bent over with age, with a tuff of wily white hair and large round glasses. He was a very simple man who had done the same thing all his life, but now he had a vision. He wanted to create something that would really make a difference in the world. He didn't think he had much time left. The year was 1998. He thought he would do something special for the new century. He would spare no expense or effort to accomplish his goal.

He painstakingly started his project. He bought the best clay he could find and chose a pearl white glaze. He bought all the hardware he would need for his project. He ordered white silk and pearls. He cleared off his worktable; this was going to take some time. He had to get it just right. He worked on his project every day, and nine months later, he was almost finished. He sculpted seven lamps. They were all about twelve inches tall. They represented different women of the world. No two were the same. One had long, straight hair and delicate features; one had curly hair and full lips; another had short hair, but they were all beautiful, and they were all pregnant. They wore long white dresses with lilies and lotuses at their feet. They each had a dove in one hand and an umbrella in the other. The umbrella held the shade for the lamp. They each had a necklace of pearls. Clara made the shades from the finest white silk. She sewed pearls around the bottom of the shades with loops to hold the crystals. Now, he needed crystals to hang on the shades. They had to be very special crystals. He traveled to Madagascar to find them, because he knew that is where the best crystals form. It took a while but eventually, he found exactly what he was looking for. He had them cut by a specialist. They had to reflect light in just the right way. He was very satisfied and proud of his work.

Able wanted to have the lamps blessed. He placed them in two suitcases, three in a small case and the other four in a larger case, carefully wrapping them in white paper and bubble wrap so they wouldn't break. He left the shades and crystals at home. He brought them to the top of a mountain so they could see the world below them. He then traveled to the ocean, dipped them in the water, and stood them in the warm sand to enjoy the sun. He set them out under the stars and left them to wonder at the universe. He took them to a forest and let them feel the rain. He watched the sunrise and sunset with them. He wanted them to be blessed by the glory of God's beautiful nature. At last, he felt that they were ready. Clara asked, "Why did you make the lamps? Because illumination brings forth the truth, said Able. Lies only survive in darkness. There was just one event left before they would be finished.

Clara and Abel were going to have a feast. They would invite their friends and family. They would showcase the lamps. As disorganized as the shop was, the house itself was very neat. It had the look of the Cape about it. Puritan-blue wingback chairs, nautical pillows, a basket of shells, and a jar of sea glass. Clara set a long table for twelve people. She used her best Wedgewood dishes and a lovely antique tablecloth, and along the middle of the table, she placed the seven lamps. She started cooking the day before the feast. She decided on the menu. They would have thin slices of cranberry walnut bread with cream cheese for an entrée on the porch and watch the sunset over the harbor. Then they would have clam chowder with oysters. crackers, Boston brown bread cooked in a can, with rich pats of butter. This would be followed by baked stuffed lobster, potato salad, and asparagus with hollandaise sauce. For dessert, they would have a luscious Blueberry cheesecake. Abel thought this was all necessary because he believed in celebrating life, your family and friends, and accomplishments.

All the guests they had invited to the feast marveled at how beautiful the lamps were. "This one is my favorite," said his sister,

Beth, who ironically had the same hair as her brother. "This should fetch a pretty penny," she said.

"These are not for sale!" he said. "They are my gift." "Gift to whom?" said Beth.

"Oh look, the entrée is ready on the porch," he said, changing the subject.

It was a warm summer evening with a slight cooling breeze. On the side table, there was a nice assortment of wines and a fruit punch. Abel helped himself to a glass of wine. "Charlie, come see Grandpa," he said, motioning to the boy with a big head of hair who was playing in the yard. "You're going to be as handsome as Grandpa someday!" said Abel. Able loved all his grandchildren but had a soft spot for Charlie. He was a sickly child and had stayed with them one summer because his parents thought the fresh air would be good for him. They went fishing every day. Skipped stones on the ocean and caught fireflies at night. They made bonfires on the beach, and Able showed Charlie some of the constellations. Able thought he was having more fun than Charlie, but he was wrong. Charlie would think back on that summer for the rest of his life.

"Dinner is served!" said Clara. Everyone filed in and took their places. They had shut off all the lights except the seven lamps down the middle of the table. He used low-watt bulbs so there was not too much light. The whole table and feast were glowing. They all stood to say grace. They said a humble prayer. Abel looked at his family and the food, and he realized how good a life he had.

"So, what are you going to do with the lamps?" said Beth.

He paused a minute, "I am going to give them to charity. They are incredibly special lamps that, under just the right circumstances, with just the right person, will cause something truly miraculous.

His sister smiled, "Well, in any case, Clara, the food is delicious, and thank you for inviting us. Abel, after dinner, let's play a game of checkers. If you remember how!" She winked at him. He knew she was laughing at him, but he did not care.

Abel didn't want the lamps all in the same town, so he decided to take a trip. He didn't want them too far away because he thought of them as his babies. He would give the lamps to different charities as he traveled around.

The next day, Clara and Able packed their suitcases and set out on their adventure. He made himself a little map. He left one lamp in his hometown of Falmouth which he did before his trip. Then he would leave one in Boston because he had a favorite restaurant that he wanted to take Clara to. They would dine on Alaskan king crab and pan-seared scallops and then enjoy crème Brule for dessert. Then they would travel to Bar Harbor in Maine, New York, North Carolina, Florida, and last but not least, Texas where they would celebrate by having a big steak and buying cowboy hats. Abel always wanted a cowboy hat. He thought it protected his head from the sun and looked cool all at the same time, not like a baseball cap that lets your ears burn.

The trip started out perfectly. They had a wonderful dinner in Boston; everything was as good as he remembered. They slept over, dropped off a lamp, then they headed off to Bar Harbor, a quaint little town on the rocky coast of Maine. There he left a lamp at the St. Jude Charity Gift Shop, then went to the West Street Café for a lobster roll. They walked around the town and did a little shopping for the grandkids. They were driving to New York tomorrow.

Abel did not want to drive into the city because he did not like the traffic, so he stuck to the countryside. They arrived in Sackets Harbor late in the evening. He found a quaint bed and breakfast. Tomorrow they will find a charity to donate the lamp to and then do some sightseeing. It was raining when they woke, so Able left his suitcases by the door and headed downstairs to sign out and have the car taken to the door. When he got to the bottom of the stairs, there was an old man who had fallen. The desk clerk and a young girl were helping him. The girl was traveling with him. He was wiggling his leg and saying that he was fine. He sent the girl upstairs to get his bags. The little drama seemed to be over.

They drove for a while, then finally found a Salvation Army drop box. He opened the suitcase, but to his surprise, the suitcase was full of men's clothes. His heart started to beat faster, and he flushed a little. *Oh no*, he thought to himself, *the cases must have gotten switched when the girl went to get the bags*. He looked closer at the case. They did look remarkably similar. He checked for some identification but found none.

"What's wrong, dear?" asked Clara.

"The lamps are gone! The suitcases got switched." His shoulders drooped. He sat on the curb.

After a few minutes, Clara sat next to him on the curb. "Listen, Able, maybe this is meant to be. I am sure that whoever those people are, they will be just as surprised as you are, and I am sure they will take good care of the lamps. Maybe the lamps were meant to go farther and do greater things than you ever imagined." They had already given out three of the lamps. The other four were gone with the larger suitcase, so they canceled New York, North Carolina, and Florida and went straight to Texas. They were not going to miss out on having a big steak and buying cowboy hats.

Chapter 2
Angie

Angie and Johnathan had rented an apartment overlooking Boston Harbor. He had gone across the street to buy fresh bagels, cream cheese, and coffee. Today was Saturday, the day she got to sleep in late and do whatever she wanted. Today, she was going to the flea markets. Then she would buy some fresh fish for dinner. Jonathan was a journalist, and she was a writer. They had met at college. It was love at first sight, which she did not believe in before it happened. She loved his sense of humor, how he laughed, that he never minded when she put her cold feet on his to warm up, and the dorky way he always kissed her hand before falling asleep, saying, "Goodnight, sweetheart." Now, she was five months pregnant and delighted with it.

Johnathan entered the apartment with keys in his hands, a bag of bagels hanging from his mouth, and two large coffees. "Oh great, I'm starving," she said as she pulled the paper bag from his mouth.

"You're always starving," he said with a wink.

She smiled back at him. It had been five years since she met him, and he still made her heart skip. "I'm going to the Quincy Market this afternoon; would you like anything?" she asked.

"Yes, fish and chips for dinner!" She knew that was what he would say

Angie tied the emerald green wool coat the best she could around her ever-expanding stomach. The Quincy Market wasn't far from their apartment. It was a beautiful day, so she decided to walk. On her way, she passed by an antique store. In the window, there was a little lamp; the base was a pregnant woman. She thought to herself, *just like me*. She went in to see the price. The inside was neat for an antique store. "How much for this lamp?" she asked the woman who was dusting off the furniture.

The woman quickly calculated the cost by looking Angie over and trying to guess how much she would be willing to pay. She had bought the lamp at the Salvation Army for ten dollars so anything over that was profit. The lamp was very pretty, and she knew it would sell sooner or later. She guessed that the green wool coat was not cheap, so the customer probably had money. "A hundred dollars," she quipped.

Angie was not planning to spend that much. She put the lamp down and wandered around the shop. She picked up a few things here and there only to put them down again. This was annoying the shopkeeper. She was superstitious and thought that the first customer of the day had to purchase something, or she would have bad luck all day. "Ok, how about seventy-five dollars? This lamp is very special," she said with a wink, "it will bring your baby good luck."

Angie smiled. She was not superstitious, but she really did like the lamp. "Sixty, and it's a deal," she said.

The shopkeeper grudgingly agreed.

Later that night, Angie was breading the fish when all six feet two inches of Jonathan walked in the door. "I have good news and bad news," he said.

"Why is it that there is never good news and more good news?" she said, smiling.

"I think it has something to do with yin and yang," he said.

"Ok, give me the good news first!" she said.

"Well, the car will be ready tomorrow, and this is the bad news." as he handed her a letter from her father.

"How do you know it is bad news?" she asked.

"Because it always is," he said with a frown.

She knew he was right, so she tossed the letter on the side table and continued cooking. She set the table with a tablecloth, a candle, and various cutlery. She never got tired of their suppers together. It was always an occasion. She knew that eventually, the baby would come, and things would change, but she hoped they would always have time for the romantic stuff. The sun was setting over Boston Harbor. The candle flickered in the light. Angie had never been so happy. Her childhood had been filled with lies and deception. She liked that Johnathan was an honest, kind, and simple person. She could not imagine him doing anything deceitful. Her father, on the other hand, was a whole different story.

When Angie was ten, her parents divorced. They did not have one of those amicable divorces where people act like grownups and put the children first. Theirs was an out-and-out battle. Angie overheard a few arguments about "that woman" and gambling." After losing custody, her father, Grant, moved to Australia to become a miner. Angie didn't see him again until she was fourteen when he sent her a ticket to fly to Australia and stay with him for the summer.

Her mother was not happy about the ticket. She was happy to have him on the other side of the planet. She didn't really want Angie to go but decided to let Angie decide. Angie didn't know what to expect but she decided to go.

This was her first time flying. The view was spectacular, and she liked the chicken dinner on the plane. Her father was leaning on a pole at the arrival section of the airport. He was wearing a Tilly hat, white shirt, and tan khakis and boots. She noticed that a few women smiled and glanced at him as they went by. One woman asked him for directions. He tipped his hat and was flirting a little. When he saw Angie, he squinted and then smiled. A child can change a lot in four years. His little girl was growing up.

Her father lived on a ranch not too far from the mines. He lived with his girlfriend, Alice, and her son, David. The woman seemed kind and the boy a little standoffish. "Why don't you go show Angie around, and I will call you when dinner is ready," said Alice.

David grudgingly complied. "Common Angie, I will show you around."

"Can you ride?" David asked.

"Well, I've never done it before; is it hard?"

"No, anyone can do it; the horse knows what to do. I will put the saddle on for you. Here, you take Ebony, and I will take Pepper."

Angie was afraid of the big black horse. He kept snorting and trying to get away from David. David tied the horse to the railing and motioned Angie to put her foot on the stirrup so he could boost her up. "What do I do when I get on?" asked Angie.

"Just hang on to the saddle and grab the reins and say, 'Giddy up, Ebony.' The horse will do the rest." David was smiling at himself. He opened the barn door and untied the horse.

Angie did not get a chance to say anything. Ebony shot off like a bullet. Angie was hanging onto the saddle pommel for dear life. Just then, Grant drove up in his Jeep. He saw Ebony heading for the west fields, with Angie. He jumped out of the Jeep, ran into the barn, and jumped on Pepper bareback. He didn't have time to saddle her up, but he was an experienced rider. When he caught up with Ebony, the horse was drinking in a small pond. Angie was walking out of the pond, soaking wet.

"Are you alright?" he asked as he checked her over. "Does anything hurt?"

"No, I'm ok," said Angie.

"Well, the water probably helped to break your fall," said Grant. "Why did you take Ebony? He is our hardest horse to handle."

"David said it would be easy," said Angie, feeling foolish.

Grant took the reins of the horses, and they started walking back to the barn. She was glad to have some time alone with her father. They talked about school, her friends, riding, and the mine. David was usually just around the corner or butting in. This time, he was hiding from Grant. She felt very comfortable with her father, even though she hadn't seen him for years. She knew in his complicated way that he loved her.

Grant wanted to show Angie the mine. They mined copper, silver, and uranium. He bought some shares a few years ago with some shady money scheme, and now they were worth a fortune. They took Grant's small plane to go see the mines. The plane ride was scarier than the big commercial flights, but it was also exciting. Grant made David sit in the back seat and let Angie sit in the cockpit next to him. When she looked scared, David leaned forward and whispered, "Giddy up," and snickered. Grant scowled at David, and he quickly sat back in his seat.

She could not believe how big the mining hole was. The huge dump trucks looked like Matchbox toys. The dirt roads winded down the sides of the mine for miles.

They landed on a small airstrip and then walked to a huge platform with a railing along the edges. Angie looked down and felt her stomach drop. It was like looking at a skyscraper. Grant put his arms around his daughter's shoulders. "Someday, my share of this will be yours, sweetheart."

Angie smiled at him, not really understanding what it would mean. Then Grant gave her a silver pen with her name engraved on it. This is so you can write to me. Grant knew he could call her, but he preferred to write. He felt that she could always reread the letters when she missed him. David glowered at Angie, wishing he could just will her over the railing and out of his life. Grant also gave a pen to David with his name on it.

The letter.

Angie sat in the big poufy chair and turned on the little lamp that she had bought that morning. She was thinking about her day. Her dinner of fish and chips was delicious. They had a nice evening. Johnathan went for a walk to help his digestion.

She opened the letter from her father. He told her another tall tale about getting into an argument with his partner, who was totally wrong to accuse him of things that were really not true. Then a fight broke out, and his partner ended up stabbing him for no reason, but of course, nothing was his fault. He was in the hospital, but when he was feeling better, he wanted to come to visit and see the baby.

Angie just sat in the chair and was thinking that she would like, for once, to know the truth. She would like to know when someone was lying and exactly what the truth was. As she dosed off, she thought she saw little lights flickering in the room then around the lamp, like a mist, and finally dancing and swirling around her stomach. It made her feel sleepy. She gave in to the feeling.

Chapter 3
Willow Brooks

Finally, the day came for Angie and Johnathan to go to the hospital. Their birth experience was pleasant. She was very surprised that it was not as painful as everyone had told her it would be. The baby was a girl, healthy but pale. She thought it was strange that the nurse said she was pale. "Aren't all babies pale?" she asked the nurse. Some are, but look—her hair is white, and her eyebrows too. We will check it out, but don't worry; it is nothing serious. The test turned out positive. Baby Willow was an albino. The doctor came to talk to them. There is nothing wrong with your daughter. She has a genetic abnormality that occurs in one out of every twenty-thousand births. She will be light-sensitive and may have trouble with her eyesight. Use sunscreen and make sure she wears a hat. Other than that, she is perfectly normal. Angie thought the doctor sounded a little curt.

"Sweetheart, she is beautiful, just like her mother. We have a daughter. Now we are a family," said Johnathan, with love in his eyes. The three of them stood in the hospital room as the light streamed in through the window. Angie suddenly remembered something her grandmother had told her long ago, "Children are not negotiable; you love what you get."

Willow was a good baby but a little fussy about meeting people. If she did not like you, she let you know. She had a strange habit of looking around your head instead of in your eyes. Her hair was white-blond, and her eyes were blue. Too much light bothered her eyes, so Angie often put a hat on her. She had a mild form of childhood arthritis and didn't walk until she was eighteen months old. She loved music, so Angie bought a book of nursery rhymes and often sang to her. Johnathan would sit in his chair and watch his wife and daughter and think about how lucky he was. They lived a charming life for two years.

Then suddenly, everything changes. Johnathan was coming back from an evening stroll. He saw the ambulance and police in front of his apartment building. His heart sank. He saw the sheet over a body on the ground. He looked up at his third-floor apartment. The patio door was open, and he could hear a baby crying. He knew that cry anywhere. It was Willow. He didn't know what to do. He thought he should ask what happened, but he was afraid to know. He saw the potted plant on the sidewalk. It looked like the one on his porch. He moved closer, his eyes teared up, and the police stopped him. "Johnathan, you don't really want to see her like that," said the policeman. Jerry was a town police officer who knew everyone in the area.

"What happened?" asked Johnathan in between sobs.

"It looks like she fell while watering the plants."

He pushed Jerry aside and knelt beside her covered body. He saw her fingers sticking out of the edge of the sheet. He gently took her hand in his and held it to his cheek. In between sobs, he managed to whisper, "Good night, sweetheart." He then kissed her hand for the last time.

Chapter 4
Moving to Westport

Johnathan found himself surrounded by memories of Angie and with a two-year-old who asked for her mother all day, every day. He just told her that her mother would be back soon. He knew he could not do this for long. He decided to move back to Westport with his father, Harold.

Harold looked like Johnathan when he was 35 years old. He had a penchant for sweaters that button up the front, with a white shirt, no tie, and a big mustache. He almost always had a pipe hanging from his mouth or in his hands. He had been very successful in the newspaper business in his younger years. He was now retired and rambled around his big stone cottage overlooking the ocean. He called it a "cottage," but it was more of a mansion. It overlooked Elephant Rock, a collection of large stones at the start of the inlet in Westport Harbor. It was surrounded by Rose Hips, a small wild rose that makes a fruit that can be made into jam and grows wild on the beach.

The home looked cold and imposing from the outside but was very warm and inviting on the inside. It had everything a large home has: a library, living room, music room, study, office, sunroom, bedrooms, four bathrooms, parlor, servants quarters, and grand entrance.

Harold was very sad for his son but delighted to have him move in. His wife, Rose Willow Brooks, had died a few years back, and he was lonely. He was absolutely in love with his granddaughter, Willow. He knew she was special.

Harold had a hobby. He loved to build clocks. He knocked down the wall in between a bedroom and the sunroom and built himself a beautiful shop. He had a very nice collection of tools, all very neatly arranged on custom cabinets. He worked on his clocks every day except Sunday. He sold some, although he really didn't need the money. He liked the thought that they were in other people's homes, adding warmth and mystery. The clocks were everywhere throughout his own house, and every clock was different. They all had carvings on them. Some were carved with roses, some birds, some willows. They all had a secret drawer somewhere and chimes. He set the time so that if you went from the library to the kitchen, you would gain twenty minutes. Johnathan argued that when you went back to the library, you would lose twenty minutes. Harold laughed and said, "There is always time to read, but dinner gets cold!" Harold had one clock in the entrance that stood still. It was a rose-carved cabinet clock, with a collection of teacups behind the glass door and butterflies and morning glories etched in the glass. It was always 3:32 in the morning. That was the time his wife continued her adventure without him.

Johnathan felt it was strange to be moving back to his childhood home. As he drove up the driveway, he looked out at the ocean. It was a cool, windy day. He did like living here when he was young, but this was a whole other thing. He worked hard, finished school, found the love of his life, had a little family, then lost everything. He re-thought that; *at least he still had Willow*. He chose a bedroom on the second floor. He put Willow in the room next to his, but he knew it would take a while before Willow would sleep more than three feet away from him.

Willow was two and a half, and she was a handful. Harold had hired a cook, Sofia, who lived in the servant's quarters with her husband, James, who was in a wheelchair. They had been married for only a short while before the doctor told them that James had ALS and it would only get worse. She was pregnant, and the job had been a godsend. They lived in the first-floor servants' quarters, so even with his wheelchair, he could still get around.

Sofia was a very good cook. Most of her recipes were Portuguese cuisine, which she got from her mother. Harold and Johnathan were hoping that Willow would like Sofia. Willow took a slow, careful look at Sofia. Then she smiled. Johnathan, Harold, Sofia, James, and Willow were now a strange but loving family. Johnathan worked every day in his office; Harold worked on his clocks, with many breaks to see how Willow was doing; and Sofia cooked wonderful evening meals that were shared by everyone. They ate dinner together in the grand dining room. Sofia decided that dinner was at six. No one dared to argue with her. James worked on his scrimshaw, a hobby he took up after getting sick. No one had the heart to tell James that he was not a good artist. Not to mention that the loss of muscle control made his art look, well . . . exotic! He felt bad that he was not able to help anymore. To everyone's surprise, his scrimshaw pendants sold well. Harold brought them to the market every couple of weeks.

Johnathan was unpacking some boxes when he came across the little lamp that Angie had bought. He thought wistfully of their past life together. He told himself to snap out of it! He decided to give the lamp to Sofia. She was pregnant, and maybe she would like the lamp as much as his wife had. Sofia was surprised but happy to receive the little gift. She gave it a special place in her colorful and warm apartment.

Every now and again, Johnathan saw the box that held the personal items recovered with his wife's remains. He could not deal with this now, so he stashed it in the secret drawer of his mother's clock. He would send her clothes to the Salvation Army because he could not bear to see them on anyone else; except for the green coat that he kept for Willow.

James, Sofia, and Jayr

James first noticed Sofia in the marketplace. She was the most exotic woman he had ever seen. He thought he was content to live alone until he met her. She had long, dark, wavy hair and a curvy figure. She was selling pork pies and Portuguese sweetbread braided with eggs. She was very friendly with all the customers, laughing and joking with the regulars. It was obvious that everyone liked her.

He also noticed that she had no ring. He would hang around the market a little and listen to the general conversations. He knew she had no one steady by the teasing from some of the old codgers that drank coffee in the market. It took him two months and eight loaves of Portuguese sweet bread until he finally got the nerve to ask her out. They married six months later, and soon after, Sofia was pregnant. She was saving up to open a little restaurant that would feature her mother's Portuguese recipes. Her dream became his.

Sofia

Sofia noticed the tall, quiet man the first time he showed up at the market. He came every Saturday and bought the same thing. He was polite and once even paid the three dollars and seventy-five cents that the woman in front of him in line was short. He had a soft, quiet air about him. After about two months of Portuguese bread and eggs, she suggested that he try the pork pies. To her surprise, he said that was a great idea, and maybe after work, she could join him in the park for a picnic. She smiled and packaged two pork pies for him. "Yes," she said, "I finish at four-thirty.

"I know," he said with an awkward smile. He thought to himself, *I wonder how long I have to wait to ask her to marry me?* He went on to buy a salad, a bottle of wine, and chocolate. He showed up at the market with a picnic basket, a blanket, and a big goofy smile.

One year into their marriage, James wasn't feeling well. He seemed to be losing his strength and coordination. He made a doctor's appointment. The news wasn't good. James had ALS. There was no cure, and it would only get worse.

After the shock and a bit of time, Sofia realized that James would not be able to work. She found an ad for a job cooking in someone's home. The job offered room and board and decent pay in exchange for light housework and cooking. Sofia applied for the job and got it. At first, it was just Mr. Brooks, who insisted on being called Harold, but they were soon joined by his son, Johnathan, and his daughter, Willow. The extra work and pay were welcome. It helped to keep her busy, with less time to worry about the future.

Sofia was sitting in a big poufy chair in her apartment, near the window, watching the sunset. She was admiring the little lamp Johnathan gave her. It made a soft glow in the room. The baby was due any time now. Her feet were swollen, and she felt that she was ready. James was sitting in his wheelchair, working on his scrimshaw. It was so hard to see him get a little worse every day. She wished she could find a cure and do something for her husband. She vaguely noticed little lights dancing in the room before falling asleep.

Jayr

Jayr Harlow was born on a cold and rainy morning. He weighed nearly ten pounds. He had dark hair like Sofia and long, slim fingers like James. Sofia and James decided on the name *Jayr* because it was an old puritan name meaning "healer." She thought maybe it would bring luck. Jayr was a very good baby, hardly ever crying unless he was hungry, but he was hungry often.

James was watching Sofia cut vegetables. The light was shining through the window. James remarked to himself, *No matter how sick*

I get, the sun will still shine. Life will go on with or without me. He was wondering how long he would be able to enjoy his family. He thought about slowly wasting away. He felt very vulnerable. Jayr was wrapped in a blanket on the counter. James rolled up to the counter. He winced as he reached over to pick up his son. "If you hold him all the time, he will get spoiled," said Sofia with a smile. She placed Jayr on his father's chest, realizing that James barely had the strength to pick up the baby. He thought to himself, *This is all I can do for my son.*

A few months later, Sofia noticed that James seemed to be getting stronger. He seemed to have more muscle control. His speech improved, his hand-eye coordination improved, and even his scrimshaw improved. He would occasionally have a burst of energy and literally race around the house in his wheelchair. Willow would hitch a ride. He would hold Jayr in one hand and use the other hand to spin the wheels. Jayr would sleep through it all.

One day, Sofia was stirring something on the stove. Jayr was standing in his highchair. He leaned a little too far back, and the chair started tipping. James was close by and saw Jayr start to fall. Without thinking, he stood up and caught Jayr. They both fell to the floor. Sofia turned around to see what all the commotion was. She saw James slowly stand on his own two feet. Jayr was laughing, thinking it was all a game. Sofia looked at James. He was a little wobbly, but he was standing! They both started laughing a little hysterical laugh that turned into tears.

Sofia made an appointment with the doctor. "Look, Mrs. Harlow, people don't recover from ALS. They get progressively worse, then they die, usually of respiratory problems. Your husband never had ALS." Sofia didn't know what to think and just chalked it up to a miracle. She was very grateful to God and the hospital and that she would have her husband back. She told herself that she would do something special for the hospital.

Time moved along smoothly like this for several years. Willow set into her little routine. By the time she was almost four, every night she went to bed in her bed then quietly snuck into her dad's She woke up and went downstairs at six and had her breakfast with Harold. He would make them toast and coffee for him, milk and cereal for her. Then they would walk to the mailbox at the end of the drive. He would collect the newspaper and any other mail. On his way back, they would play "Which hand is the candy in?" He would hold out his two hands, palms down, with a candy in one hand. "Which hand Willow?" She would smile, close her eyes, then say, "That one, Grandpa," and every single time she was right.

Willow Turns Five

Willow was very excited about her birthday. She was turning five. Sofia was baking her a cake. Willow and Jayr were sitting on the counter, watching her. Willow was waiting for Sofia to finish the batter because she wanted to lick the beaters. "Did you buy me a present, Auntie Sofia?" she asked with a shy smile.

"I don't buy presents for silly, counter-sitting, batter-licking, endless-talking little pests," said Sofia, with a big smile and a kiss on Willow's forehead.

Willow smiled, "I'm going to take good care of her," she said.

Sofia looked surprised. "You little rascal, did you snoop in my room?"

"No," Willow said quietly, "I saw you buy her."

Sofia was trying to think back to when she bought the doll and whether Willow could have been nearby. Suddenly, Jayr fell off the counter. He landed headfirst with a big smack on the forehead. Sofia could see the lump getting bigger by the minute. She went to the freezer and got a bag of frozen peas. "Here, sweetie, put this on your head. It will take the boo-boo away."

Willow thought that Jayr looked funny with the bag of peas on his head. She started giggling, and then Jayr started giggling. "I want a bag of peas, too," said Willow.

"I only have one bag, sweetie," said Sofia.

Jayr said, "Here, let's share," and handed the bag to Willow.

"Jayr, you got a good bump there. Keep this on your forehead," said Sofia. While she was putting it back, she noticed that the lump had disappeared. "Well, it was not that big a bump after all," she said. Sofia finished the batter and gave them the prized beaters.

Chapter 5
The Visitor

One day the whole family went to Boston Gardens to hear a concert. It was a free concert; they would have a picnic in the park, and they would all go for dinner afterward. It was going to be a treat from Harold. They all piled into Sofia's old van. Harold looked stressed about the van because it was old and sputtered when it was started, but Sofia pointed out that it was the only vehicle they would all fit in. Harold had a sports car, Johnathan a Jeep. Sofia packed a wonderful picnic of pork pies, Portuguese sweetbread, and shaved asparagus salad.

It was pouring rain, so Sofia brought a colorful array of umbrellas. It rained all the way to Boston, but as soon as they entered the park, a large hole opened in the clouds, and the sun shone through. Just before the concert started everyone was surprised and delighted by a magic show performed by a young boy. He was making cards dance to music. "I really can't figure out how he does that," said Johnathan. Another boy who was with the young magician passed around a hat. Harold put in ten dollars. "Well worth it," he said to the young man. They found a nice place for their picnic.

Later, they all enjoyed the concert and the lovely dinner that followed. When they got home, they were surprised that the front door was open. Johnathan entered first and looked around. He didn't see anything out of place. They all entered, thinking that perhaps they had not closed the door properly and the wind had pushed it open. When Sofia entered her apartment, she realized that someone had been there. There was a plate of leftovers on the table next to the poufy chair. Whoever it was did not steal anything other than leftovers, and they thought it would be strange to call the police for leftovers. They told themselves that they would lock the doors more often. Harold smiled at that.

On this particular morning, they had just finished their little walk down the driveway. Harold was delighted to have received a catalog of clock hardware.

"Grandpa! Can you play cards with me, please?" said Willow. He looked at his granddaughter with her yellow raincoat, duck boots, and a big smile.

"Well, do you know any card games?" said Harold.

"Yes, Go Fish!" she said with that little smile that he could not say no to.

"Ok, sweetheart. Let me get a few puffs on my pipe, and then I will play Go Fish with you."

Harold could not smoke in the house anymore because Sofia would not allow it. He puffed his pipe a few times on the porch then entered the house. Willow had already set up the cards.

"You can start, Grandpa," said Willow.

"Do you have a four?" asked Harold.

"Go fish!" said Willow.

"Do you have a five?" Willow.

"Nope, go fish," said Grandpa.

Willow looked at him, closed her eyes for three seconds, then said, "Grandpa! You do have a five."

"How did you know that I had a five?" asked Harold.

"I just close my eyes, and I can see your cards," said Willow.

Harold laughed. "Wouldn't that be a great trick?"

One day, Willow was playing with one of the many cats that seemed to hang around the house. Harold had made her a cat toy with a piece of string and a pompom from an old hat. Jayr, Sofia's son, was sitting on the floor with a big tabby purring on his lap. Willow and Jayr were two years apart, but they were the same height. Jayr loved animals, and they loved him. He was always carrying a stray cat or bird or frog around with him. When he went outside, the animals would follow him. Jayr followed Willow everywhere. They made a strange parade of animals and children. Today, they were running through the house with two cats in tow. They went to Harold's shop. He was working on a new clock. They knocked on the door. "Grandpa, can we come in?" asked Willow and Jayr in unison. Jayr considered Harold his grandpa, too.

"Sure, come in, but don't touch any switches." Harold set up two pieces of wood, some small nails, and two finishing hammers. "Here, see if you can bang these nails in." He thought that would keep them busy.

Willow saw a piece of chain hanging out of a cupboard. She went over to see what it was. She pulled on the chain, and it turned out to be a necklace with a scrimshaw pendant. She noticed that there was a whole box of them. "Grandpa, can I have one?" asked Willow.

"Me too, Me too," said Jayr.

The two kids were rummaging through the box of pendants. "No, I'm sorry but those are not mine. Come and finish your projects and we will go for ice cream after, Ok?"

Jayr was very content with the thought of ice cream. Willow looked at her grandpa with a sad face. "Oh, sweetheart, what's the matter?" Said Harold.

Willow hesitated for a few seconds, then she said, "That is not true; they are yours. You bought them." Harold looked surprised. He was trying to figure out how she knew. Maybe she overheard someone talking about it. He pretended to sell the pendants because he felt sorry for Sofia and James when he was sick and knew they could use the money, but how did Willow know?

Chapter 6
The Picnic

It was Labor Day weekend. Willow was going to start first grade soon. She was very excited about going to school and making new friends. It was a very hot and muggy end of August. To celebrate the end of summer, they were going to have a moonlight picnic. Sofia had James and Johnathan lug an old picnic table onto the beach. They set up torches and beach chairs, and Sofia made a wonderful picnic of shrimp chorizo and roasted pineapple kababs, spaghetti squash with tomato and fresh cheese, and Berlin balls for dessert. The party would not start until sunset.

Willow and Jayr both took a nap in the afternoon. They all changed into bathing suits and coverups. Willow was glad that she didn't have to wear a hat or sunscreen because it was getting dark. Harold wore his sweater over his bathing suit although he had no intention of swimming. The red-and-white checkered tablecloth stood out in the moonlight. The soft, warm wind made the torches sway while the light from the moon was dancing on the water. They were all enjoying the sumptuous meal that Sofia had prepared. Sofia and James were talking about opening a little restaurant someday, now that James was well. She would use her mother's recipes like they had planned. Johnathan was a little sad to hear the news but was glad for them. "To new endeavors," he said, and they all made a toast.

After devouring the Berlin balls while licking her fingers, Willow said, "It's time to swim." The kids threw off their coverups and took off running. Johnathan, Sofia, and James chased after them.

"Wait for us," they said, "It's dark, and there is an undertow." They made a chain, holding hands as they ran into the warm, salty water. Johnathan held Willow's hand, and she held on to Jayr. Harold opted out of swimming, as he had planned, and just sat on the beach and smoked his pipe. Sofia and James waded in slowly. It was an enchanted evening. Willow felt a strange sensation that went from her hands to her shoulders and through her body. She stood still for a moment. Jayr was jumping up and down with the waves. Willow started jumping, also. After a while, a few clouds passed by the moon, and it got darker. It was time to pack up and head back to the house.

They packed up the picnic stuff and snuffed the torches. Jayr had already fallen asleep on the beach chair, but Willow was full of energy. She grabbed her coverup and started running back to the house. Johnathan looked at her, amazed and happy to see his daughter run. From that day on, Willow ran every day.

Colors and Numbers

Willow loved first grade. Her teacher, Mrs. Applebee, was going to teach her how to read! She was just so excited. She could not wait to read all the interesting books that Harold had in the library. She was learning colors, numbers, and letters. Her life was very exciting.

Sofia had sewn an outfit for Willow that looked like the one Willow's doll was wearing. A traditional Portuguese outfit, with an embroidered vest and full skirt, a white shirt with puffed sleeves, and a straw hat with a flower on it. She insisted on wearing it on the first day of school.

"Don't forget your glasses," said Sofia.

"I don't need them anymore," said Willow with a smile.

Sofia put the glasses in Willow's school bag.

Willow made a friend, Jane, who had red hair and freckles. Jane wore a princess costume with a fireman's hat and a cowboy's lasso. They had their lunch together. Jane had a baloney sandwich with cheese and chips. Willow had pickled sardines and green apple salad. Willow looked at her lunch with dismay. It didn't smell very good. A few of the kids started laughing at her. Willow threw the salad in the garbage. Mrs. Applebee asked her to throw it in the outside garbage, and then she gave Willow half of her baloney sandwich. They both shared Willow's Orange-thyme pound cake.

After lunch, Jane and Willow tried to lasso a fire hydrant. Suddenly, a man approached. Willow looked at him and started screaming. "Run, Jane, he is dark."

They both ran back into the building. Jane thought it was a fun game. "Let's play that again?" said Jane.

"No," said Willow, "he scares me."

After school Sofia asked Willow how her day went. Willow didn't answer but asked, "Can I have a ham sandwich tomorrow?"

"You didn't like your lunch?" asked Sofia.

"No," said Willow, very honestly. "It didn't smell good, and the kids laughed at me."

"Oh, I'm sorry, sweetheart," said Sofia. "Sardines are not everyone's favorite." The next day, Willow had a Black Forest ham sandwich with Havarti cheese.

Later that week, Mrs. Applebee was absent; they had a substitute teacher for a day. When Mrs. Applebee came back, she had a bruise on her cheek. She had tried to cover it up with makeup, but it still showed.

They were all sitting in a circle on the floor on a reading carpet. Mrs. Applebee picked out a book and read it to the class. When she finished reading, Willow raised her hand. "Yes, Willow," said Mrs. Applebee.

"How did you get hurt?" asked Willow.

Mrs. Applebee put her hand on her cheek. After a few seconds, she said, "I fell off a ladder while painting."

Willow looked at her in a strange way. She stood up and walked right up next to Mrs. Appleby and whispered in her ear. "Please,

Mrs. Appleby, don't let him hurt you anymore."

Mrs. Appleby's started to tremble then started crying. She left the room. Just then, Sofia and Jayr were approaching the school. Sofia came to pick up Willow. The class could see them out of the window. A squirrel jumped down from a tree and approached Jayr. He knelt to pick up the squirrel. "Don't touch him," said Sofia. "That is a wild animal."

The principal came into the room to try to settle the children in class down. "Ok, children it is almost three, time to pick up and collect your things."

Bubbles and Other Troubles

It was a nice Saturday morning. Willow, Jane, and Jayr were all playing around the rosehip bushes. Jane found a bottle of bubbles under the picnic table. "Let's make bubbles," she said, but when she opened the bottle, there was no wand.

"That's Ok," said Willow, "I know where to get one." She ran into the house and into Harold's shop. She knew she was not supposed to enter his shop when he was not there, but it would only take a minute. She ran to the little rack that Harold kept all his pipes in. She grabbed the corncob pipe and quickly left the shop. Willow banged the pipe on the picnic table to knock out all the old tobacco. Then they poured the bubble mixture into it. To their delight, it worked. They each took turns making bubbles and chasing after them to pop them until Sofia called them in for lunch.

Sofia was practicing her recipes for her restaurant. She made them a Roasted Potato Salad with Roasted Leek Mayonnaise and

Cod with Green Peas and Poached Eggs. For dessert, they had a Pear Almond Pie.

After lunch, Willow and Jane went back outside to play. Jane found a little bird under a bush that was hopping on one leg. She was able to pick him up. "Look, Willow, I found a bird," said Jane.

"I think his leg is broken," said Willow. They put the bird back on the ground, but it just sat there. "Let's show Jayr," said Willow. They brought the little bird into the house.

Harold was just coming out of his shop. "What do you have there," asked Harold.

"Jane found a bird with a broken leg," said Willow. "Jayr is going to fix it," she said with confidence. Harold smiled. Ten minutes later, Harold went outside for a smoke just in time to see Jayr place the bird on the ground. The bird walked a few steps, then flew off. Willow smiled at Harold. Harold was glad to let Willow believe in miracles. He knew she would grow up someday.

Later that afternoon, Jane's mother came to pick her up, and Jayr fell asleep on the big chair in the entrance hall. Willow was going to watch Sofia cook supper. She loved the fast and efficient way that Sofia cooked. There was always some interesting scrap to taste. Harold spotted her on the way toward the kitchen and said, "Wait, Willow, did you see my corn cob pipe anywhere? I seem to have misplaced it.

Willow said, "No," and ran out of the room. Willow wanted to watch Sofia, but she suddenly had a horrible headache. "What's wrong?" asked Sofia. "Are you alright?"

"My head hurts," said Willow, starting to tear up.

Sofia felt Willow's head. She didn't have a fever. "Maybe you should take a nap before dinner," she said.

Willow knew what to do. She went to see Harold in his shop. She knocked on the door. "Come in," said Harold. Willow walked up to Harold. "What's up, sweetie?" he asked.

"I took your pipe this morning," she said. "We wanted a wand to blow bubbles." She looked down at her feet. "I'm sorry; I know I should have asked."

Harold smiled at the thought of the three of them blowing bubbles with a pipe. "Well, thank you for telling the truth," Said Harold.

"I have to tell the truth," Said Willow. "Lying gives me a headache."

"That is probably your conscience," said Harold.

Chapter 7
Strange Event

The whole school was in the gym watching a basketball game. Jane, Willow, and Jayr were sitting together. Willow had to use the bathroom, so she got permission and went. On her way back to the gym, she saw a little girl about her age running down the hall. The girl pulled the fire alarm! Then without saying anything, she ran out of the school and down the embankment and got into a car. The alarm was blaring.

The teachers calmly led all the kids out into the playground. Just then they heard the roar of a small airplane. It was flying fast, and there was smoke coming out of the wing. It came closer and closer. Mrs. Applebee saw the danger and warned the kids to run to the end of the field. Just then, the small plane hit the school. There was an explosion. Bricks and glass were falling everywhere.

Soon, fire trucks arrived with the police in tow. It slowly dawned on the teachers that whoever pulled the alarm saved their lives. Mrs. Applebee thought it was Willow. She was the one in the hall when the alarm went off. Everyone else was accounted for. "Did you pull the alarm, Willow?" asked Mrs. Applebee.

"No, it wasn't me. There was a girl in the hall; she pulled the alarm and then ran out of the school."

Mrs. Applebee just smiled; she was sure it was Willow.

Christmas Miracle

It was getting close to Christmas. Sofia was very grateful that her husband was cured. Even though the hospital didn't seem to know how he was suddenly cured, she felt that she should do something for the staff over the holidays like she had in years past, so she baked enough Suspinos Meringue kisses to fill a hundred boxes to give to the children's ward at the Jordan Hospital in Plymouth. James had gone there because they had a specialist for ALS. This year, she took Willow, Jane, and Jayr with her to help give out the boxes. It was going to be a fun day.

Everyone at the hospital knew Sofia. A few of the nurses helped her with the packages. They piled them on a little table in the hall of the children's ward. Despite that it was a hospital, there was a festive atmosphere with decorations and a tree. Sofia and the girls started giving out the meringue kisses while chit-chatting with the children. Jayr wandered off down the hallway.

Sofia and the girls gave out all the boxes. The nurses bought eggnog, and they wished everyone a merry Christmas. That's when Sofia found Jayr sleeping on a chair. She tried to wake him up, but he was fast asleep. She picked him up, and they went home.

After a few days passed, Sofia thought that Jayr might have caught something. He was sleeping too much. He would wake up to drink a little and then fall back asleep. She decided to take him for a checkup.

They were sitting in the doctor's waiting room when a man with thick dark hair came in. He was having an Asthma attack. He sat in a chair and leaned back. He was slowly trying to draw a breath. His wife was with him. She gave him his inhaler, and he did his best to breathe deeply.

Jayr walked over to the man and started playing with the man's watch. Then he held on to the man's hand for almost a minute. Sofia and the man's wife were busy talking to the nurse. When Sofia saw what Jayr was doing, she called him over. "Don't bother him," said Sofia. The man with the big hair just smiled. The inhaler was kicking in. The man was feeling a lot better.

Just then the nurse called, "Jayr Harlow." Sofia and Jayr went into the doctor's office. They took some blood and other tests but could not find anything wrong. We will send in the samples and get in touch with you, but he looks healthy to me, said the doctor. Sofia was annoyed and said, "But look, he is sleeping again! That's not normal."

"He must be going through a growth spurt or maybe not getting enough sleep at night," said the Doctor. "Does he watch a lot of television? Does he have a regular bedtime?"

Sofia was insulted. She thought that the doctor was implying that she was the kind of mother who let her kid watch too much TV and had no regular routine. She left the office annoyed. As they were passing through the waiting room, the nurse called out. "Charlie Smith, room two, please."

The next day, the hospital called Sofia to let her know that a vile of Jayr's blood had gone missing, and they wanted her to have another one taken. She decided not to go again. Jayr seemed fine, and the Doctor was rude.

Two days later, Harold was reading the newspaper. The headline was "Miracle in The Children's Ward." He called out to Sofia, "Hey, did you hear all the children in the children's ward at the Jordan Hospital were released today? They tested everyone! One of the patients had leukemia, another cancer, yet another a spinal cord injury, one had a broken leg . . . and everyone was cured.

"Let me see that," said Sofia. She read the article. In the article the nurses said that it was "Sofia's Suspinos kisses that cured them." Sofia smiled. Then she started getting orders for her meringue kisses. Hundreds of them. She had so many orders that she had to rent a professional kitchen to bake them. They all pitched in and when the craze was over, Sofia had enough for a down payment on her restaurant.

Police Station

Sofia had errands to do, and Harold had an appointment, so Johnathan took Willow with him to the police station. He was researching an article on police and racism. He was interviewing a police officer that just been acquitted in a shooting.

"Good morning, Johnathan," said Martha, the receptionist. Martha was one of his neighbors. She was a kindly older woman.

"Good morning," said Johnathan. "How is the fishing?"

"Good, I'm going this afternoon. I'm going to catch myself a big one," said Martha.

"I hope you do," said Johnathan. Martha smiled. "Can Willow sit here with you for a few minutes while I interview Officer Peter Stone? The Commissioner said that Officer Stone was willing to cooperate. It shouldn't take more than a half hour," said Johnathan.

Martha cleared off a space on her desk and made a place for Willow. She gave Willow a large box of crayons. "Here, sweetie, draw me a picture," said Martha. Willow pulled up a chair. Just then Officer Stone came into the room. The officer noticed Willow sitting in the chair. "What a pretty girl you are," said Officer Stone. Willow just stared at him. She moved a little closer to Martha. He bent over closer to Willow and asked her name. Willow slid off her chair and ran to Johnathan, and hid behind him.

"Willow, you stay with Martha, and Officer Stone and I are going to talk at that desk?" said Johnathan as he pointed to the other side of the room. Willow reluctantly obeyed, making sure to stay far away from Officer Stone. Willow drew a picture for Martha. She drew herself, Martha, her father, and Officer Stone. In the picture Martha was smiling with a big fish. Her father had a pen and paper in hand and was taking notes. Willow was standing next to her father, and Officer Stone had a gun in his hand and was pointing it at a black man who was shot on the floor in a pool of blood. Willow had drawn a black zigzag around the head of Officer Stone. She drew white zigzags around everyone's head, but Officer Stone's was black. Willow gave the picture to Martha. Martha looked surprised. It was a gruesome picture for such a sweet-looking little girl. Martha gave the picture to Johnathan.

Once they got back to the car, Johnathan asked Willow about the picture. "So, what is that?" said Johnathan, pointing at the big fish.

"That is the big fish that Martha wants to catch," said Willow.

"And what is that?" asked Johnathan, pointing at the man on the floor.

"That is the man that the policeman killed," said Willow.

"How do you know that? How can you possibly know that?" asked Johnathan.

"I told you, Dad. I close my eyes, and I see the truth. I saw Officer Stone shoot the black guy, who was crying. Officer Stone is a dark person," said Willow.

"What do you mean by dark?" asked Johnathan.

"Most people have light around their heads, but some are dark. They frighten me. The policeman is dark, the postman is dark, and Jane's father is dark," said Willow very seriously. Johnathan was very disturbed by what Willow was telling him. He didn't really believe her, but there was no other explanation for what she said. He investigated a little more into Officer Stone's reputation. He did have other shootings, and they were all black men.

Johnathan waited until after dinner. He brought Willow into his office. Harold was in the corner in his favorite chair, reading the newspaper. Willow was still eating a leftover Suspinos, meringue kiss. These had slivers of nuts and chocolate, and Willow thought they were divine. Johnathan sat in the big leather chair. Willow climbed on him and sat on the armrest. "Willow, what do you mean by you close your eyes, and you see the truth?" asked Johnathan."

"I can tell when someone is lying. I close my eyes, and I see what the truth is like in a video clip. The truth is blue. If someone tells a lie and they know they are lying, I see red in the light. If they think they are telling the truth, there is blue in the light. If someone is good, they have light around their head; if they are bad, they have darkness around their head. Daddy, can I have a Bella Bird for my birthday?" asked Willow, changing the subject completely.

"What is a Bella Bird?" asked Johnathan.

"It is a toy. I found a shop online called Robert's Boberts. He sells special toys," said Willow.

"What kind of bird?" asked Johnathan. "It has multicolored feathers, and it talks and hovers."

"You mean like a drone?" asked Johnathan, a little distracted. He was still thinking of what she said earlier. "How old are you now . . ." he said teasingly, "five, oh, I mean six?"

"No, Daddy, I'm seven," said Willow.

"Ok, I guess you are old enough for a Bella Bird."

Willow skipped out of the room. Harold put down the paper for a minute and looked at his son. "Knowing the truth can be very dangerous," he said.

"I know, Dad, I know," said Johnathan.

Chapter 8
Willow's Birthday

S ofia made a *tarte de bolacha* Maria for Willow's Birthday. She bought multicolored balloons with helium gas in them and blowouts with whistles. She invited Jane to the little party. Sofia wanted to do something special for Willow because she was going to open her restaurant soon, and she would be leaving. She found a nice building that had an apartment upstairs and a place for a restaurant downstairs. It was overlooking the harbor. She felt bad that she was moving out, but it was time to move on with her life. She made Willow's favorite supper: lobster rolls with fresh vegetables and a *presunto* and cheese-stuffed bread loaf for an appetizer.

Even Jayr insisted on buying a gift for Willow. He was now five years old. He went with his father to buy the gift. He was very happy with his choice.

They all gathered around the table. Sofia had set candles and used the good China. After dinner, they all played pin the tail on the donkey and then tag hide and seek. Jayr kept losing because he kept whistling on his blower, so the girls found him right away.

Then it was time for the gifts. Johnathan gave Willow a pretty wrapped box. "Oh, my Bella!" said Willow delightedly. "Thank you, Dad," She opened the box. It contained a pretty bird with multicolored feathers. It had to be programmed. Johnathan sat down with the directions. He noticed that at the end of the directions on how to program the bird, it said. "DO NOT OPEN, DANGER."

Jayr gave his gift next. Willow was pleased to have another gift. It was two little bottles of Penelope's Potions. The bottles were very mysterious looking. "Thanks, Jayr," she said with a wink. "I will try them in school tomorrow. They were having a little party at school to celebrate the opening of the new gymnasium.

"Here you go, Willow," said Johnathan.

Willow took the toy and said, "Hello, Bella!"

The bird replied, "Hello, Willow."

"How old are you?" asked Willow.

"I am three minutes old," said the bird. Then she pushed a little switch, and the bird started flying. It flew exactly three feet off the floor. It had a little leash, and Willow pulled it around the room. Jayr and Jane followed her.

The New Gymnasium

The next day was just half a day of school. They would only have one class, then a party in the new gymnasium. There were balloons, party sandwiches, punch, coffee, and various bowls of chips. Mr. Holland, the principal, had ordered cupcakes for everyone. He was a tall man with a large head and a serious nature. They were going to be in the newspaper tomorrow. A cameraman was coming to take pictures.

The new gymnasium had all the gadgets, even a trampoline, all the sports equipment you could think of, the whole nine yards. Everything was shiny and new. The teachers and the principal were all sitting in a circle in one corner of the room. Music was playing. Willow and Jayr went over to the coffee pot and dumped one of the potions into it. Then, they went over to the punch bowl and put the other potion in.

After a while, Mrs. Applebee motioned to everyone that they were going to start the dance. Music for the *Hokey Pokey* started playing. "Put your right foot in!" said the principal, then he started giggling like a three-year-old. He put his large hands over his mouth, but as soon as he tried to talk, he started giggling. Then Mrs. Applebee farted loudly! Then other people started giggling and others farting until the whole room was either giggling or farting. Just then the cameraman entered the room. Even he was laughing, as he was taking pictures. He was also holding his nose. Willow, Jane, and Jayr found the whole thing very funny. "Hey Jayr, best gift ever," said Willow, giving him a high-five.

Harold was laughing while drinking his morning coffee. "Hey, Johnathan, look at this." On the front page of the newspaper was a large picture of the new gymnasium with the principal with his hands over his mouth, Mrs. Applebee looking embarrassed, and everyone either holding their nose or laughing." The headline read: "New Gymnasium Stinks."

Sofia's Kitchen

On the way home, they stopped at a corner store. It was an old store that had a little bit of everything for sale. Boots, chips, gum, soup, ant traps, and other miscellaneous items. Sofia was looking for the cream of tartar and batteries. Willow saw a small, mysterious-looking rack at the back of the store. It had potions. This must be where Jayr bought the potions he had given her. They had Turn Back the Time potion, Run Again, Fart Attack, Love Story, Truth Serum, and Giggle Pills. There were also Big Hair and Remember Me pills. She knew she didn't need the truth serum, so she asked Sofia for the Big Hair. Sofia thought it was funny, so she bought it.

Early the next morning, Willow was sleeping in her room when she heard a noise. She thought that maybe her father was getting a glass of water. She pulled the blankets closer and fell asleep. She woke up to the sound of Bella saying, "DO NOT OPEN! DANGER." But she was hearing it outside. She ran to the window just in time to see a small explosion in a black SUV parked in the street. Two men in black jumped out of the car. They were blue! Their hair, faces, and clothes were stained blue. One of them started laughing at the other, then realized that he was blue, too. They both got back in the car and left. Then Willow realized that Bella was gone. They must have taken her. The next day Willow emailed Robert's Boberts to let him know what happened. Robert was glad to know and said he would send another Bella with a warning system, free of charge.

Chapter 9
The New Cook

W illow was moping around the house. She went into Sofia's old apartment. It looked strange with the furniture and Sofia's things gone. The only thing left in the room was a sewing machine. The house felt empty without Jayr. She was used to seeing him every day. Willow went to see her father in his office. "Dad, can Jane come for a sleepover?" she asked.

Johnathan lifted his gaze and looked at Willow. He knew she was lonely. "Sure, that's a great idea. Call and see if it is Ok with her mother, and when I finish this, we will go pick her up," he said. Willow skipped out of the room, happy with her plans.

They picked up Jane and stopped for ice cream on the way back. Johnathan had taken the top of the Jeep, and the warm wind was melting the ice cream. Jane and Willow had trouble licking fast enough. When they got home, there were two cars in the driveway. One was fairly new, but the other was a beat-up Buick. There was a young man sitting in the old car reading. Harold was interviewing cooks. Since Sofia left, they had been eating a lot of pizza and frozen dinners, and Harold wanted some real food. Jane and Willow went to sit on the front stairs. A young man got out of the car. He was dressed in blue jeans, a rumpled denim shirt, and brown loafers. His blond hair was neatly combed, and he had blue eyes. Willow thought he looked like an angel. He looked too young to have much experience, at being a Chef. Willow was thinking that her grandpa would not be impressed. The young man walked up the step and sat next to Willow. "Hello, I'm Daniel. What's your name?" he asked.

"I'm Willow, and this is Jane," said Willow with a smile. Just then the front door opened, and a woman came out. She smiled at Willow and got into her car. Harold was right behind her. He lit up his pipe and looked out at the ocean. "Well, just one more interview," he said, "but I think I have made up my mind." Just then he noticed Daniel.

"Hello, I'm Daniel. I'm here for an interview for the cook's job." He held out his hand, "Nice to meet you."

Harold shook his hand. "You look awfully young to be a cook," said Harold.

"I'm eighteen, sir, and someday I am going to learn how to cook at Le Cordon Bleu in Paris."

Harold looked a little skeptical. "Well, can you cook now?" asked Harold. "Why do you want a job here?" he asked.

"Because it comes with room and board," he said bluntly.

"Don't you have family?" asked Harold.

"No," said Daniel.

Harold puffed on his pipe. "What kind of food can you cook?"

"Anything you want," said Daniel.

Harold took a few more puffs on his pipe. "Ok, I will give you a chance. Tonight, I want beef Wellington, mushroom gravy, roasted garlic potatoes, green beans, and a Charlotte Ruse for dessert. I have an account at the IGA on Lincoln Street. You can buy what you need there. If I like the dinner, you can have the job."

Daniel smiled and thanked him for the chance. Daniel got into his old Buick, and with a puff and a backfire, he jerked out of the driveway and drove over the curb. "I hope he cooks better than he drives," said Harold. "What do you think of him, Willow?" asked Harold.

"I like him," she said.

"Was he telling the truth?" asked Harold.

"No," said Willow. She saw that Daniel's father was a violent man and had kicked him out of the house. His mother gave him money in an envelope. He was living in his car.

Harold was startled. "What was he lying about?" asked Harold.

"His family," she said. "But he really doesn't have anywhere else to go."

Daniel returned with bags of groceries. Willow and Jane showed him the kitchen. Daniel was busy opening drawers and figuring out where everything was. Then he went to his car and brought back a duffel bag, a pillow, and some blankets. He opened his bag and pulled out a rather rumpled cook's hat and white jacket. Wow, he looked like a real cook! Jane and Willow were very impressed. They watched him dice onions very evenly and rub spices on the beef before searing it and covering it with the crust. "Jane, let's set the table," said Willow. The two girls set the table for six people.

"Who is the sixth place for?" asked Daniel.

"It's for you. We all eat together."

Daniel was a little nervous. He thought the green beans were a little undercooked. The beef Wellington looked superb. He arranged the food on a large platter surrounded by vegetables. A large gravy boat held the delectable sauce. In the middle of the table stood the Charlotte Ruse.

Daniel took his hat off and took a place in between the two girls. They all took turns serving themselves. "Take some vegetables," said Johnathan to Willow with a smile. They all said grace and started eating.

Daniel was watching Harold. Harold took a slice of Wellington. He looked at the doneness of the meat and the browned crust. He dipped it in the gravy. He quietly savored the mouthful. "Very good, Daniel," he said with a smile. "However, the green beans are a little too crunchy."

"I know," said Daniel. "I was a little nervous."

Willow looked at her grandfather with an anxious look. "Grandpa, look at that dessert!" said Willow.

"I will make a pot of tea," said Daniel and left for the kitchen.

"Please, Grandpa, choose Daniel," whispered Willow.

Daniel came back with a pot of tea and served the dessert. Finally, Harold pushed his chair back a little. "Thank you, Daniel, for a very good meal. You are hired," he said with a smile and a wink to Willow. It was obvious that Daniel had nothing but what he had in his car. "There is some furniture in the attic that you are welcome to use," said Harold. "Willow will show you where it is."

Willow, Jane, and Daniel headed to the attic. The stairs were in the hallway on the second floor. It was one of those traps in the ceiling that you pulled down. The attic held a large assortment of furniture from different eras. Some were covered with sheets, some not. Willow, Jane, and Jayr had often played in the attic. Harold had traveled with his wife, Rose, and they had collected various things from their travels. There were maps, ornaments, an old easel carved with roses, clothes, chairs, bedroom furniture, frames, mirrors, et cetera. Jane found some maracas and started playing with them and dancing around.

"Wow, this place is amazing," said Daniel. He pulled the sheet off a bed frame, sending up a pile of dust. "Great, I can really use this," said Daniel. There was a big chest in the corner of the attic. They slowly opened the chest.

"Hey, this is my grandmother with Grandpa when they got married," Willow said, showing a picture to Daniel and Jane. There were boxes of mementos, postcards from all over the world, a few lovely scarves, a box of coins, and an old set of tarot cards. Willow picked up the box of coins. "Oh, I like this one she said," picking out a coin and holding it to the light.

"Look at this," said Daniel as he picked up the mysterious cards.

"I bet this is worth something," said Willow, interrupting Daniel.

Meanwhile, Jane was dancing around with the scarves. Her long red hair was shining in the moonlight, streaming through the dormer window. "Oh, this place is magical," she said with a sigh.

"Hey, let's go downstairs, and I will read your fortunes," said Daniel.

"How are you going to do that?" asked Willow.

"With these mysterious cards, of course," said Daniel.

They took their treasures downstairs. Just then Johnathan entered the room. "Hey girls, it is getting late, time for bed."

"Ok," said Willow, "you can read our fortunes tomorrow, Daniel."

Jane's Secret

Jane and Willow had had a big day. They put on their pajamas and slipped under the covers of Willow's double bed. Willow and Jane were giggling and eating some green potion pills. The moon was shining through the window. Willow was telling a scary story about a ghost from the attic. Jane was not impressed. Just then Johnathan came into the room to tuck them in. When Johnathan approached the bed, Jane slid under the covers. "Good night, girls," he said and pulled the covers under Willow's chin. He gave Willow a kiss on the forehead. Jane was still hiding under the blankets.

After he left, Willow looked at Jane. She was very quiet. "Jane, my father would never hurt you. You didn't have to hide." Jane started crying. Willow hugged her. "You have to tell your mother what your father is doing," said Willow. Jane said nothing for a moment. "Just tell her, "Said Willow.

"I can't," said Jane. "I am afraid."

"Promise me you will tell her," said Willow. Jane nodded yes.

The next morning, Harold found Daniel sleeping on the sofa in the entry. Daniel was curled up with an old blanket and a pillow, and he looked like he was twelve. Harold sighed to himself. He went to look in the apartment. Daniel had installed the bed from the attic, but there was no mattress. He had brought down a globe, a large dresser, a mirror, a bird cage, an easel, two chairs, a map of Europe, and a small table. In the corner he put a desk with Sofia's sewing machine. Harold ordered a mattress and sheets for Daniel from Sears.

The two girls came down the stairs laughing and giggling at each other. Their hair was standing on end like they had stuck their fingers in a socket. Jane tried to push her hair down, but it went right back up. They found Daniel sleeping on the sofa.

"Wake up, Daniel, we want breakfast! Waffles and strawberries and chocolate milk."

Just then Johnathan walked into the room. "Good thing you girls don't have school today!" said Johnathan, smiling.

Daniel made the delicious breakfast that the girls asked for. "What did you do to the coffee?" asked Harold.

"You don't like it?" asked Daniel."

"No, it is wonderful. I want this every morning!" said Harold with a smile.

"Cheers," he said, clinking his cup in the air. Daniel was starting to feel more comfortable. "Do you mind if I borrow some books from the library?" he asked Harold.

"Sure, what kind of stories do you like?"

"Sherlock Holmes. I noticed that you have a large collection."

"Yes, my wife, Rose, loved them."

"Thank you," said Daniel, "I will be very careful with them."

After breakfast, the girls went into Daniel's apartment to have their fortunes told. Having no clue as to how to tell a fortune, he had Willow pick out five cards. He slowly placed the cards on the table in a row. "I see that you are going to be very notorious!"

Willow just smiled, "That's not true," she said, "you are just guessing."

"Read my fortune," said Jane. Daniel looked at the cards, "Hmmm, you will be moving suddenly, and for the first time in your life, you will feel safe."

"That is true," said Willow, quietly.

Redecorating

The next day, Johnathan had some business in town. "Will you be Ok with Daniel and Grandpa after school?" he asked Willow.

"Sure, Dad, Daniel is going to make homemade pizza pockets, and he said I can help."

Willow went to see Harold. "Grandpa, can we redecorate the living room? We found some cool stuff in the attic," she said."" I guess so,". Said Harold," just don't make a big mess." Thanks, grandpa, you're the best!" said Willow.

Harold was working in his shop. He kept hearing the sound of furniture being moved around. He ignored it for a while then decided to take a smoking break. He was surprised and dismayed at the huge mess Daniel and Willow had made. "Where are the curtains?" asked Harold."

"I took them down to wash," said Daniel, "and I thought I would freshen the paint while I am at it. I found some really cool stuff in the attic!" He said with delight in his eyes.

Harold did not know what to say. He sighed deeply and headed out to the porch. That night, they all sat around the table and ate pizza pockets. Harold looked at his supper. Pizza pockets. He was thinking to himself, this is not what he wanted when he hired a cook. To his delight and amazement, the pockets were delicious. They were a little bit spicy, with just the right amount of cheese and vegetables and a delightful crust. He helped himself to another one. They had ice cream with homemade chocolate fudge sauce for dessert.

Willow helped Daniel clean up, and since it was Friday and there was no school tomorrow, she stayed up and helped Daniel with the decorating. Johnathan had a few errands to do after supper. He smiled when he got home. Willow and Daniel were painting, laughing, and listening to music. The room looked a mess, but the kids looked happy, and it was time for a change.

The next day, it was quiet. Harold could hear Willow and Daniel talking in Daniel's apartment. He opened the door slightly, just enough to see Willow perched on a large chest and Daniel sitting at a desk sewing. He saw what was left of the heavy tweed living room curtains. *Oh God*, he thought to himself.

"Hi, Grandpa," said Willow, smiling. "Look what Daniel is doing. He is making shades!"

"The coffee is ready," said Daniel, "just the way you like it."

"Thanks," said Harold, with fake enthusiasm. Harold wandered off to get some coffee. He decided that he would go to the village today and have lunch at Sofia's restaurant. Harold invited Willow to have lunch with him, but she wanted to stay and help Daniel with the decorating project.

When Harold got back, he was amazed. The room looked great. Daniel had made shades that could be opened by pulling on a string. They did not cover the windows so much, and the light streamed through. They had painted the walls a very light taupe and rearranged the furniture. There was a subtle picture of Sherlock Holmes in a Paris setting that Willow's grandma had bought many years before, over the fireplace. Daniel had put the collection of books on the mantel with brass bookends on each end. There was a collection of pipes arranged in a shadow box on the wall. There were light-colored pillows and soft throws on the sofas. Daniel had arranged the furniture to make a nice, comfortable seating arrangement in front of the fireplace. He put candles in the fireplace for a warm glow. He had put some tall ferns in the corner and brought down an old phonograph. Soft music was playing old French songs. A tea cart held a collection of teacups and some crystal decanters. There was a picture of Harold and Willow Rose on their wedding day on a side table. Harold didn't know what to say, so he said nothing. He got himself a drink, sat on the sofa, watched the flickering candles, and listened to soft music. It was both painful and comforting to feel his wife's presence.

The next day, Harold and Johnathan were sitting on the porch. They had just had a wonderful meal of baked cod and blackberry cobbler. Harold was smoking his pipe and Johnathan was sipping on his tea. Daniel and Willow were inside, busy playing with the old piano in the music room. They were making a racket, so the two older men had escaped to the porch. "Does Willow ever ask about her mother?" asked Harold.

Johnathan hesitated for a minute. "No, not really. I don't know what to say. If she asked me, I would be lost for words," said Johnathan.

"She must wonder," said Harold.

"Yes, but she was so young. It was so tragic. There was no reason, just a freak accident. I don't want her to think something like that could happen again," said Johnathan with worry in his voice.

Just then Willow and Daniel came through the door at the same time, nudging each other over a little. Daniel was wearing a deerstalker. Johnathan smiled to himself. Daniel looked very serious. He sat on the porch step and pulled out a corn cob pipe. Then he proceeded to take out a small pouch of tobacco. He dumped a little bit of tobacco into the pipe. Then he tried to light it. Harold saw what he was doing. "You have to pack it in solid," said Harold. "Look, like this." He took the pipe and pushed the tobacco into the pipe more firmly. "Now puff a few times to light it. There you go."

Johnathan could not believe that his father was showing a Sherlock Holmes wannabe how to smoke a pipe. "You know, Sherlock Holmes never really wore a deerstalker," said Johnathan."

"Yeah, I know, but it is so cool," said Daniel, very seriously. Johnathan just started laughing. Harold looked up, wondering what was so funny. "Nice hat, kid," he said.

The Coins

"Grandpa, what do you think this is worth?" asked Willow as she held out one of the coins they found in the attic.

"I don't know, probably not very much," said Harrold. "Rose was an avid coin collector, but I doubt that any of them are valuable."

"Can Daniel and I go to the jeweler on Lincoln Street and see what it is worth?

"Sure, have fun," said Harold.

"Dad, can I go with Daniel to the jeweler's today to get the coin appraised?"

"If it is Ok with your grandpa, it is Ok with me," said Johnathan. "Hey, does Daniel have seatbelts in that hunk of junk car?" asked Johnathan.

"I think so, but he will drive very slowly," she said with a smile and a hand gesture.

Daniel drove very slowly out of the driveway. They were on an adventure and didn't want to get stopped at the beginning. They found the address for the coin shop and parked the car. The car was parked with one wheel on the curb. They entered the little shop. There was a big man at the front desk. "What can I do for you today?" he asked.

"We have this coin we would like to have appraised," said Willow. Willow handed him the coin.

He took the coin in his hands and looked at it. A look of delight flashed across his face. "Well, I will have to look closer in my shop with a magnifier. I will be back in a moment," said the shopkeeper. The large man went into the back of the shop. A few moments later, he returned with the coin. "I am sorry, but this coin is worth a dollar. There are millions of these."

Willow looked at him. She said nothing. She wandered around the shop. "Daniel, I want this fountain," she said. There was a fountain that was in four pieces. It was rather large. "This will look great in the front yard."

Daniel was trying to imagine the fountain in the front yard. "Are you sure?" he asked.

"Yes, it is perfect."

"Do you think it will fit in the car?" asked Daniel.

"I am sure it will," said Willow.

"That costs $50 dollars," said the shopkeeper.

"Pay him, Daniel," said Willow. Daniel whispered to Willow that that was all the money he had for the week.

"Trust me, said Willow quietly. Daniel paid him. Then Daniel and the shopkeeper started loading the fountain into Daniel's car. While they were busy, Willow slipped into the back of the shop and retrieved the coin that the shopkeeper had hidden in a little box under the counter and replaced it with the coin that the shopkeeper had given her. They drove off with a fountain in the car. Willow was sitting in the front seat with a smug look on her face. "Daniel, this coin is worth $30 thousand dollars," said Willow.

"How do you know that?" asked Daniel.

"The shopkeeper told me," She said with a smile.

"Dad, Dad!" said Willow, running through the front door. "The coin is worth $30 thousand dollars, and we have a fountain!" Willow was breathless with delight. Daniel followed her less enthusiastically. Harold and Johnathan were at the entrance. "What have you two been up to?" asked Johnathan.

"We had the coin appraised. It is worth a lot, and we bought a fountain. Well, we had to buy the fountain to distract the shopkeeper, but it is a nice fountain; it will look great in the front yard." Willow convinced Harold to pay Daniel for the fountain. Harold had the coin appraised by a reliable appraiser, and it turned out that the coin was very rare and really worth almost $30 thousand dollars.

Chapter 10
Mary Sue and Billy Bob

Mary Sue lived in a small town, in the middle of nowhere, with almost no opportunities. She was one of the forgotten children. The ones who never got a chance. She was very small, pretty, sweet, and very likable but poor, uneducated, and outwardly unimportant. Everyone in town thought she was great until the school bus accident.

Billows Creek was a very religious town. When Mary Sue lost a leg, everyone just assumed that that was what she deserved because God would not let that happen if it were not deserved. So, she had no choice but to accept it.

There was a little restaurant at the end of the town called The Last Chance Café. It was built sometime in the '50s. It still had the tabletop jukeboxes that you put a dime in to hear music. It had red checkered curtains and Formica tables. You could not find a gas station for another hundred miles. Mary Sue went to the café every Friday night. She would watch the girls dance and flirt with their dates. She would drink coffee and read. Mary Sue loved to read. She got a list of the classics and was slowly reading through all of them.

Billy Bob was very tall. He looked like Gaston in the movie *Beauty and the Beast*, so his friends often called him "Gaston" to tease him. One night, Billy Bob Walker was sitting on the other side of the café watching Mary Sue. He heard all the rumors. He noticed that even with a missing leg, the guys still hit on her. She just politely sent them away. One night, he got up the courage to ask her to dance. He walked up to the table and said, "Can I have this dance?" and held out his hand. She thought he was making fun of her. She glared at him. "I Hope You Dance" by Lee Ann Womack was playing. She looked at him straight in his eyes, "I can't dance," she said.

He paused for about three seconds and said, "Yes, you can." He very gently picked her up by her waist, balanced her on his hip, and started to waltz around the room with her. Everyone stopped moving; all you could hear was the music and the rustle of his feet on the floor as he waltzed Mary Sue around the room.

They got married two weeks later. He painted the little house that his parents had left him a beautiful pale yellow. He did not have that much to offer her, but he loved her. One of her aunts sent a gift for their wedding. It was a beautiful lamp with a white shade and crystals. Mary gave it a special place in the small house next to the wood stove, where she put the comfortable chair where she would read.

Billy Bob fixed cars for a living. He had a garage in the back of the house with a big painted sign on the front that said, "Billy Bob's

Garage" in big red and blue letters. He built a tall fence to hide the mess; he had a lot of stuff back there. When one of his sheds was full, he would just build another shed leaning on the existing sheds to make more space. He kept everything because he had nothing. Still, the front yard was pretty, with flowers and trees and a stone walk up to the front door.

When Mary Sue was about eight months pregnant, she was sitting in her chair, calculating the bills for the garage. "We seem to be having less work lately," said Mary Sue.

"I know," said Billy Bob. "The cars are starting to be more complicated. I don't always know how to fix them."

She looked at him with a loving glance. "It's Ok, sweetheart, we will be fine." She wished that she understood how cars worked, how anything worked. She didn't even know how the fridge worked. She thought she saw little dancing lights as she slowly fell asleep.

Finally, the baby arrived. Mary Sue found it very hard to move around while pregnant with crutches and was relieved to finally have the baby. It was a boy. Mary Sue insisted that her son would have a real name. Something serious, something that would give him a better chance in life. She was sitting in the car at the pharmacy waiting for Billy Bob to park when she saw a truck go by that said "ROBERT" in big letters. She thought it was a sign. "Let's name our son 'Robert,'" said Mary Sue.

"I thought we would name him Billy Bob Junior," said Billy Bob.

"Well, Bob is short for Robert," said Mary Sue.

"No, Rob or Bert is short for Robert," said Billy Bob.

Mary Sue smiled. "No, it is like the name Dick, it is short for Richard," said Mary Sue.

"No, Rich or Ard is short for Richard," he said with a smile. "Let's call him Ard!"

Robert was a mischievous child. He played with everything, touched everything, and he followed Billy Bob everywhere. Billy Bob just laughed it off. Mary Sue just worried that he would hurt himself. Robert was mesmerized by the garage. By the time he was four, he was not strong enough, but he knew how to fix a car. Robert understood how everything worked. He understood electricity, gravity, space, magnetic currants, black holes—Tesla had nothing on him.

Billy Bob's garage got to be the place to go to fix your car thanks to Robert. Whatever was wrong, Billy Bob's garage could fix it. He started getting fancy cars from the city. The garage's reputation grew, and he got more and more successful. Robert quit school in the third grade to work with his dad. Robert would tell his dad how to fix things, and Billy Bob would do it. Robert was built small like his mother. He had blond hair like his mother and green eyes. He stood up very straight like most short people do. This did not cause him any lack of self-confidence. Robert and Billy Bob built an addition to the house. They built a beautiful library for Mary Sue. It was built the same way the garage had been expanded. Billy Bob just added a big library right beside the small kitchen. Then he painted it the same pale yellow with white shutters. The library was four times bigger than the whole house. It was two stories high and had sliding ladders and beautiful wood bookcases, large windows, and a skylight in the middle. Needless to say, it was the talk of the very small town.

Robert's Bobberts

Robert decided to sell toys to make some extra money. He invented a toy with a gravity manipulator as a major component. This was a device that could manipulate gravity. It could hold an object at a certain height indefinitely. Let's say you wanted something to hover three feet from the ground; well, you could adjust the gravity manipulator to do just that. He decided to sell them online. He also invented a device that would destroy the object if tampered with and spray out blue ink. He knew that this invention would someday be very valuable. He knew that he should get a patent, but he also knew that the patent office flagged any patent that had anything to do with free energy, cars that run on water, or anything that upset the system. Their inventors soon disappeared. He liked living, so he didn't bother with the patent. He figured a patent just tells people what you are doing so they will have a chance to stop you.

One of his first clients was someone called Willow Brooks. Robert made a cute bird that could hover and talk and had colorful feathers. He also built a turtle and a skateboard. The turtle could be sat on and pushed around. The skateboard was very fast because there was no friction. It had wheels, but they were just for looks. Robert liked to go to town and show off his skateboarding skills.

Robert had a friend named Buddy Brown. He was the next-door neighbor, but still, he lived two miles away. Buddy was always in a good mood, to the point of distraction. He was talkative and polite. He would say nice things to all the grownups he met and was just as kind to his friends. He was genuine about what he said but it sounded fake because children usually don't talk that way. He had red hair, as did his whole family.

Robert and Buddy became friends in first grade. After school, Buddy would come to see him at the garage. They would spend hours tinkering on new inventions. The potato gun was one of Buddy's favorites.

Buddy had a sister, Brenda, that Robert had a crush on. He gave a Bella bird to her when he was invited to her birthday party. Brenda's father was cooking barbeque in the backyard. He didn't like Robert very much. He was sure that Billy Bob was doing something illegal. He couldn't understand where all the money was coming from. He saw the huge addition that Billy Bob had added to his little house. He didn't like Robert's self-confidence; he thought he was a showoff. He was very curious about the Bella Bird. Brenda was thrilled with it. She was pulling the bird around the yard.

The next day, Robert went to pick Buddy up on his skateboard. He was signaling wildly in the window. It looked like he was telling him to go away. Robert didn't understand, so he rang the doorbell. Buddy's father, who was a very big man, answered the door. He was not happy, and he was blue! It took three seconds for Robert to figure out what happened. Buddy's father slammed the door.

The Invention

Robert waltzed into the kitchen with his usual air of confidence. Mom, sit there and don't move for a few minutes. Mary Sue smiled at him. He was always up to something. He pulled off her slipper and started making a cast on her leg. He made her a cup of tea while it was drying and gave her the latest book she was reading, *Rebecca*. Then he carefully cut off the cast. He gave her a quick kiss on the cheek and disappeared into the magical garage. The garage was truly magical for Robert. He could find most of what he needed to build his inventions, and what he couldn't find, he would order online and pick up at the post office. Mary Sue and Billy Bob, on the other hand, had no idea how to use the computer. Mary Sue did try. Eventually, she could find recipes and news. Robert figured out how to get internet even in the country and had set up a strange sort of energy collecting system that gave them free electricity.

A few weeks later, Robert came into the kitchen with a grin. "Mom, I have a surprise for you." Mary Sue was sitting in the beautiful library in her favorite chair. "Look," he said with pride. In his hand, he had a leg. It was skin-colored with a movable ankle and brace that would be used to fasten the leg to her body. "Here, try this on." He adjusted the brace. "How does it feel?" he asked.

"It feels very snug," she said.

"Stand up, try to walk," said Robert.

She stood up, a little wobbly at first. She put her hand on Robert's shoulder and took a few steps across the room. "Hey, I can walk—without a crutch!" She hugged him. She looked down at her two feet. "Hey, you even painted the toes!" Then she started to giggle. It nervously turned into a hearty laugh.

"What's so funny?" asked Robert, unsure of her reaction.

She laughed a bit more; just then, Billy Bob came into the room. "What's going on here?" he asked, wanting to join in on the fun.

Mary Sue was crying and laughing. "Ha, Ha, Ha! I have two left feet!"

Billy Bob looked at her feet, and sure enough, both feet were left feet. After a few minutes, Mary Sue was walking around the room. "Thank you, Robert, it is the best gift I have ever had."

Robert smiled; he realized his mistake.

The Beatle

Robert was really excited. Someone had given his dad an old Beetle "bug" car. It was turquoise and still had the flower vase. It was a little beat up but was the perfect base for what Robert had in mind. Buddy Brown was super impressed.

"Wow, that is a lovely car," said Buddy. "You are a great Dad to give your son such a lovely car," said Buddy.

Billy Bob just smiled. He was used to Buddy by now. "Robert, just don't get into trouble," said Billy Bob. "You know how your mom gets."

Robert was looking at the car; his mind was racing. This is not too big; I think my gravity manipulator will work well on this. Buddy said, "I like you, Robert, you are my best friend."

Robert smiled. He was used to Buddy's unwavering kindness by now, too.

It took a couple of months, but the boys finally finished revamping the car. It was time for a test run. They had just finished having lunch. They opened the large door to the wonderland of a garage in the back. They closed the door. Robert had picked a daisy from his mother's garden on the way in. They painted the Beetle robin's egg blue. Robert had turned the front seat around so the seats faced each other. He built a little table in the middle and installed the flower vase. He plopped the daisy in the vase. He had installed a bunch of switches and buttons on the table. The two boys were sitting in the car. "High-five," said Buddy with a big smile. With a slap on their hands, the boys were off.

Robert had left the wheels on the car for aesthetic reasons, but the wheels were not really touching the ground. They both looked out of the side windows. "Full speed ahead," said Robert. The car shot off sideways into the field. The cattails were banging on the side of the car.

"Lift her up!" said Buddy.

Robert slowly pushed the makeshift gear, and the car rose higher. "Don't pass by my house," said Buddy. "My father is still mad about the blue incident."

"I think we will stay in the fields for a while," said Robert. The boys spent the afternoon zooming around and seeing what the car could do. They passed through a swamp and the mud was flying everywhere. The little blue car was now brown. As they flew higher and higher, they could see the mountain that they lived on. They were both taking in the view when suddenly the window shattered, and glass was flying everywhere. Buddy screamed, "Oh my God!"

Robert dived down to avoid disaster. Just then Robert spotted Mr. McConnell with his duck-hunting rifle. "He thinks we are a bird," he chuckled as he dove down under the trees.

Mr. McConnell sent out his dogs to find the big bird. Robert circled around the property and headed up the driveway. He made sure to drive straight ahead instead of sideways so as not to upset his mom. Mary Sue was looking out the library window when the boys drove up. "Oh, you finally got it going; good for you," said his mom. "Remember, you don't have a license, so you can't leave the property."

"Yes, Mom, I know," said Robert with a sigh.

New Client

Robert had just finished lunch when a black SUV drove up the driveway. Two men got out of the truck. They were both large men in black suits. Robert thought they looked like the guys in *Men in Black*, the movie. They said that they heard that Billy Bob's garage could fix anything. Robert went to get his father. When he was gone, the two men were snooping around.

The guys seemed very curious about the garage. Robert showed them where they could sit while they worked on the car.

"Why aren't you in school?" asked one of the men.

"Oh, my teacher is sick, and she had no replacement today," said Robert.

"So, what's the problem?" asked Billy Bob.

"I think it is the alternator," said one of the men. The other guy was wandering around the shop. He was trying to see in the other section of the garage where Robert kept his Beatle. Robert went and closed the door.

"What's back there?"

"said one of the men. Nothing, just junk," said Robert a little too quickly.

One of the men started whistling. "What's this? he asked as he picked up an odd-looking object.

"That's my potato gun," said Robert proudly.

"Do you have a license for it?" asked one of the men.

Billy Bob started laughing, "Yes, it is right next to my fishing net license!"

The two men smiled. Robert went over to the SUV and leaned in next to his dad.

"Go get me a new alternator," said Billy Bob.

Robert went to get one but came back with something else in his pocket. They changed the alternator, and at the same time, Robert put one new thing in the SUV. He placed it carefully so the men wouldn't notice. Robert was smiling to himself.

"We heard in town that there have been some strange lights in the sky around here. Have you ever seen anything?" asked one of the men. Robert realized that someone must have seen the Beatle's headlights the last time he went for a drive at night with Buddy. They went out at night so they would not get shot down like the last time.

"Nope," said Robert. "We also heard that a toy exploded, a toy that you brought to a party." Robert realized that they had been talking with Buddy's father. "Where did you get that toy?"

"I bought it at the flea market," said Robert. "Do you have a receipt?"

Billy Bob was smiling.

"No, it was a flea market!" said Robert.

"I think that should do it," said Billy Bob.

"Here is my card," said one of the men as he gave a card to Robert. Billy Bob thought it was strange to give his son a card. "If you see or hear anything strange, give us a call." The card was black with a gold emblem in the middle. In the square, there was a SIS. Robert smiled at the men, and they left.

The two men were driving down the road. As soon as they hit 40 miles an hour, the truck started quacking. "Where is that coming from?" Said one of the men in Black" "I don't know. "Said the other. "What did you do?" I didn't do anything! The two men looked at each other. We're going to have to keep an eye on that kid! Then they quacked all the way home.

Chapter 11
Lulu

---

ulu lived on the side of a mountain in Africa. Her father brought tourists on safaris. They had a modest home perched on a huge rock. Their world was shaken when her mother died suddenly. She said she didn't feel well and was going to take a nap. She never woke up. Then her father started making plans. She could hear whispering in the night when she was supposed to be sleeping. She heard them say, "She will be fine. She is fifteen now, old enough to marry her off to a good husband. You don't have to worry about her."

"We are family," said a deep masculine voice that she did not recognize. "Tambo needs a wife. He has two children, and his wife just died."

She heard her father say, "I want Lulu to have this house and my land. She has worked side by side with me and my wife for years."

"A woman cannot own land," said the deep voice. "We will take care of her. Don't worry about anything. Just take care of yourself."

A year later Lulu's dad told Lulu that in the morning they were going to town. This was a big event because they did not go to town often. "Take everything that means anything to you," said her father. He held out a duffel bag. Lulu wasn't sure what he meant but the seriousness in his voice gave her a clue. She packed her clothes, a few mementos, a picture of her mother and father, and a picture of Africa from the view of the front porch. They drove into town. It took a whole day. Lulu leaned against her father. He held her hand.

They arrived at a small airport and entered a small restaurant. They ordered coffee, and then Lulu's dad said, "Lulu, you must listen very carefully. You cannot stay here. I am sick; I don't have much time left. As soon as I am gone, my family will marry you off and take everything away from you. A woman can't own land here. So, I sold my land.

I have the necessary papers for you to go to America. You have enough money, if you are careful, to give you a good start. I bought you a ticket. You are going to live with my sister in New York. She knows you are coming. This is the only way you will have a chance of a good life." His eyes were glistening.

"Dad, I don't want to go," she said with tears in her eyes.

"I know you don't, but sweetheart, it is the only way."

The small plane was leaving soon. Lulu hugged her father for the last time. She looked into his eyes. She saw the love he had for her. She saw hope and strength, and his strength bolstered hers just enough to enable her to board the plane. The small plane jerked off of the runway, heading for the larger airport that would eventually bring her to America.

Lulu arrived in New York and saw a young man in the airport waiting with a sign that said "Lulu Agrinya."

"Are you Lulu?" he asked.

"Yes," she said.

"Then follow me," he said. She was not sure if this was a safe idea, so she just stood there. "You come with me!" he said. She just stood there. "Hey, girly, you come with me!"

"Who are you?" she asked.

"I am here to pick you up, and I don't have all day. Your aunt sent me."

"My name is not 'girly,'" she said, "it is Lulu Agrinya."

"I know that. It is on the sign," he said with annoyance. "The longer it takes, the more it will cost your aunt. It is up to you. I can just sit here and watch the birds."

"Are their birds in the airport?" asked Lulu as she looked around in amazement.

The young man looked at her with exasperation. "Are you coming or not?"

"What is my aunt's name?" asked Lulu.

"It is half blind, crabby pants, Adesia Agrinya," said the surly young man. Lulu reluctantly went with him.

They arrived at a small apartment in New York. Adesia lived on the second floor of a rundown apartment building. When they arrived, the young man held out his hand for the payment. Adesia gave him one twenty- and one ten-dollar bill. "Where is the rest?" he asked. "You said thirty dollars, and you only gave me twenty," Lulu whispered in her ear that she had given him thirty. Adesia gave him another ten dollars and closed the door.

"Why did you give him another ten dollars?" asked Lulu. "Because it is worth knowing who I can trust and who I cannot," said Adesia.

Lulu and Lilly

Lulu found the city to be very noisy. The honking of the cars, the sirens, and the overall street noise were strange to her. She was used to the quiet of the African plains. The beautiful starry nights. She wondered why there were no stars in New York. "There are stars," said Adesia, "but you can only see them occasionally when there is not too much pollution or light." Lulu took comfort in the fact that Adesia looked like her father. She was kind, gentle, and wise. She wore really thick glasses. She was affectionate with Lulu. She would braid her hair and cook the kind of food that Lulu was used to eating when she was young. The apartment was very small but neat. Adesia put a single bed in the living room for Lulu. There were three locks on the front door. Lulu wasn't used to locking the door. In Africa, they closed the door to keep the animals out. Adesia said that it was almost the same thing.

Two weeks later, Lulu started school. She felt very out of place. She knew no one. She was sitting alone at a table in the lunchroom when a girl approached. She was a streetwise girl who seemed very sure of herself. "Can I sit here?" she asked. She was not really asking, just stating.

"Sure, none of my friends showed up today," said Lulu with a smile.

"Great, I'm Lilly," she said as she put down her tray. Lulu just looked at her. She was blond with a slim build, but she gave the impression of being tough. "What are you doing after school?" asked Lilly.

"I am looking for a part-time job," said Lulu.

Lilly just looked at Lulu with a smile. "They are always looking for staff at the hotels. It only pays minimum wage. Do you have papers?"

Yes said, Lulu.

Lulu and Lilly became good friends. They had a ying and yang kind of friendship. Lilly was bossy, brash, tough, loudmouth, impulsive, and endearing, but most of all, loyal. Lulu was deliberate, quiet, contemplative, careful, and forgiving. Lulu found a little library not too far from the apartment, where she could read. Lilly had no use for books but liked the hot chocolate at the bookstore and would occasionally use the old, clunky computer. Lilly felt an odd need to protect Lulu from her surroundings.

Post-Graduation

When Lulu graduated high school, she got a second job at a nearby coffee shop. That is where she met Stuart Wilson. He came in every day with a briefcase. He would order coffee, two eggs, bacon, toast, and marmalade. Lulu thought that it was strange to have the same breakfast every single day. She thought if she had the choice, she would try something different every day. He was very polite. He was always doing some sort of paperwork. When she came over, he would stop whatever he was doing, give her all his attention, and place his order. Then he would ask her how her day was going. She never knew what to say. She would just smile. She didn't know if he was really interested or was just being nice. He was white as paper; she was dark as granite.

One day, he entered the coffee shop while she was not looking. She was on a break and very studiously working on something. He glanced over her shoulder. She was working on a sudoku puzzle. Lulu loved numbers. She wished she understood them more. She knew enough to understand that all of nature worked with numbers. The universe, medicine, plants, statistics, geometry—all had to do with numbers.

"Put a six there," he said, looking over her shoulder.

"Hey, it works!" she said with delight. She turned to look at him.

"'Shakespeare in Love' is playing tonight at the cinema. Would you like to go?" he blurted out clumsily.

She looked around shyly. "Ok, I will ask my aunt."

Later that evening Lulu asked her aunt if it would be Ok to go to the movies with Stewart. "I am going to have to meet him," said her aunt. "You have him come in, and I will decide then."

Lulu did not think that was a good idea. "What kind of guy would you say yes to?" asked Lulu.

Adesia leaned back in her chair. She quietly thought for a minute. "I just don't know; I would have to meet him."

Lulu was sure that Adesia would not approve. Stewart was very different from anyone Adesia knew.

That evening, Adesia was sitting next to the window when she heard a commotion. She looked out the window in time to see a man trying to steal a handbag from an elderly woman. A young man interrupted the exchange and got a punch in the face for his trouble. The thief did not get the bag, and the older woman just hobbled away in fear.

The next day Stewart knocked on the door to the apartment. Lulu let him in. Adesia looked him up and down. "Humm," she said. Stewart was standing there, being judged by an old woman he didn't know. He was getting irritated. Adesia just smiled. She recognized the young man with a black eye. She knew she could trust him. "You two go have fun, but just remember, I know when the movie finishes and just how much time it takes to get back here!"

That is when Lulu's love of movies started. She loved the big screen. The in-your-face action of the whole event. The sound, and drama. The bigger-than-life feeling. It made her feel alive. She clapped at the end of the movie. Stewart smiled. She was the only one who clapped, but she didn't notice. She stood up and continued clapping. Stewart joined in. Lulu smiled and took his hand as they exited the cinema.

They went back to the apartment. Lulu and Stewart played cards while Adesia took a nap in her bed with the door open. For all his talents with numbers, Stewart could not win a game of cards if his life depended on it. Stewart had a good job at a real estate firm.

From that point on, Stewart and Lulu spent all their spare time together. This went on for six months. One night, Stewart was getting ready to leave the apartment. Adesia was snoring in her bed with the door open. He took Lulu in his arms. "I can't imagine living my life without you," he whispered in her ear. There was a silence. Lulu looked up at him.

"Well, then get married," said Adesia from her room.

Stewart and Lulu just started laughing.

The Wedding

Lulu and Lilly went shopping for a white dress. "Nothing says it has to be a white dress," said Lilly.

"Yes, Adesina says it has to be white, so it will be white," said Lulu.

They were rummaging through the piles of clothing at the Salvation Army. Lilly had two dresses in her hands. "Hey, Lulu, if we take the top of this and the bottom of that, I think it will work."

Lulu took a look. "Can you sew?"

"Sure, I can," she said with a smile. "I can do anything that I really want to do." With that, the girls headed home, happy with their findings.

Later that night, Adesia adjusted the dress because it turned out that Lilly finally found something that she couldn't do.

The day came for the wedding. Adesia insisted that Stuart and Lulu get married at the church that she attended. Lulu had gone every week since she arrived in America. She loved the enthusiasm that the singers had for singing and God. It was so lively and vibrant. You could not help but feel enthusiastic.

Stuart contacted his family to let them know that he was getting married. His father refused to come because of Lulu's race, but his mother said she would do her best to attend the wedding. On the day of the wedding, Stewart's mother arrived at the church alone with a gift.

It was supposed to be a small wedding with a cake and champagne-like drink after. It turned into quite the event when all Adesia's friends brought food. Everyone danced and sang and celebrated with the young couple. Lulu and Stewart were happy. His mother was kind and did her best to excuse her husband for his absence. She bought them a beautiful little lamp. She told Lulu that it would bring light into their lives. They rented an apartment just over Adesia's. Lulu wanted to keep an eye on her aunt because she felt grateful toward her and had grown to love her like a mother.

They took a trip to the Cape for their honeymoon. They ate fried scallops overlooking the bay, they rented scooters on Martha's

Vineyard, and they watched the sunset on their way back from Nantucket on the ferry. Lulu had never been so happy.

After the honeymoon, Lilly and Lulu painted and redecorated the small apartment. Lilly announced that she was going to marry her high school sweetheart, Edward. They had a little party. Stewart and Edward got along well. They worked on the same street, so they carpooled to work. They would have get-togethers for football games and any other events. Lilly showed Lulu how to cook American food.

It was not long before Lulu and Stewart decided to start a family. Stewart had a good job, so she quit working at the hotel job and just kept the waitressing job. Lilly and Lulu painted the spare room with a big "Welcome to America" sign on the wall. She found navy blue sheets with stars on them for the crib. Adesia sewed a quilt with the American flag, the Statue of Liberty, and patriotic sayings, all red, white, and blue. Lulu was grateful for the new start in America and the new life that was coming.

Lulu had framed a picture of their wedding day for Stewart to bring to work. He proudly put it on his desk. He was looking at it when his boss came in. "Stewart, we are promoting someone to be the manager, and we are considering you for the promotion."

"That's great," said Stewart.

"We need someone responsible, reliable, and aligned with the company."

"That is me," said Stewart. He stood up, and his boss came over to the side of the desk. His boss saw the picture.

"Who is that?" he asked.

"That is my wife," said Stewart with a smile.

His boss just glared at the photo. "Well, I will get back to you about the situation." And he quickly left the room.

Stewart went home happy about the news and told Lulu that he was in line for a promotion. They celebrated with tea and chocolate. The next day, Stewart was fired. They escorted him out of the building. He didn't know what happened. He thought over the day. *What went wrong?* He didn't even see his boss. The security guards followed him in and out. He stood on the street. He didn't know what to do. He started walking home with his box of personal belongings in his hands. He had a few files, a stapler that he had bought, and a picture of his wife. How was he going to explain this to Lulu?

They were both disappointed but were trying to be optimistic. Stewart tried to get a job in his field but seemed to be blacklisted everywhere he went. He finally found a job in a completely different field in James Bay, Canada. He would be gone for weeks at a time, but at least he would be employed. Money was getting very tight. Lulu was sitting in the neat apartment, working on a sudoku puzzle and thinking that she wished that she understood numbers better. Lulu still had some money left that her father had given her. She would have liked to invest the money in the stock market but didn't understand how it worked. She turned on the little light next to her chair. She took a deep breath. Somehow, this will all work out, she thought to herself. She saw little lights dancing in the room and fell asleep.

Lilly's Wedding

Stewart was in James Bay during the wedding. Edward was from a large Italian family, but Lilly was an only child raised by her mom. Lilly loved the feeling of belonging to a large family but was not used to all the attention. The aunts all wanted her to have a big, elaborate wedding. Lulu and eight relatives went wedding dress shopping with Lilly. Edward's four sisters, Fiametta, Allegra, Zanobia, and Rosanna; his grandmother Donata; two of his aunts, Antonella and Paxe; and last but not least, Bela Flore, his great-grandmother. They wanted her to wear a tiara, gloves, and carry a huge bouquet. Lilly was in the dressing room. Lulu was watching the whole spectacle. They were all fussing around her.

"Oh, this one really suits you," said Antonella as she plunked a tiara with flowers and jewels and a sparkly fabric veil on her head.

"Oh, look," said Aunt Paxe, "This dress will make your small chest look more. Ah, womanly," she said, smiling slightly, as she held up a dress with more ruffles than Lilly thought was possible to put on a dress.

"She doesn't need that," said Fiametta," "but look at this bouquet; it is just perfect!"

"That bouquet is bigger than she is," said Zanobia. "Maybe she can push it down the aisle on a cart!"

Lulu started laughing.

Bela Flore piped in, "In my day, a girl carried her own bouquet; there was no such thing as a cart! But you know, I could use a cart to carry me right about now."

"Good idea. Let's go for lunch!" said Lilly. "I'm' starving, and if I don't eat soon, my womanly chest may disappear!"

Paxe smirked. "Yes dear, good idea."

They went to a restaurant nearby that was owned by one of the aunt's relatives. The food was delicious. They had a Caprese salad and a sumptuous risotto with focaccia bread with olives, and sundried tomatoes. This was all followed by gelato and, espresso and grappa to finish off the meal. Everyone was satiated and getting a little tired.

"This was fun," said Aunt Paxe. "Let's do it again next Saturday." All the aunts agreed.

Lulu smiled at Lilly and whispered, "Tomorrow, you and I will go shopping alone." They winked at each other.

Lilly walked down the aisle in a lovely, simple-fitted white dress with a boat neck. Some of her hair was braided with pearls, and the rest hung down straight. She had a Lily of the Valley bouquet. Lily of the Valley had a special meaning for her. Lilly's mother told her that when Eve was exiled from the Garden of Eden, her tears dropped to the ground, and from them grew a simple, small white flower. That is why she named her Lilly. Her mother was superstitious and religious and believed the name would bring her daughter luck in love. She had read somewhere that the Lily of the Valley signified the return of happiness, something she really wanted for her daughter. Her father left when she was very young. Lilly's mother died two years earlier from breast cancer. Lilly always missed her, but it was times like this that she missed her the most.

For the rest of the afternoon, into the evening there was lots of dancing and singing and celebrating. Everyone loved the tough little woman who was marrying the adored Edward.

Chapter 12
The Birth

Lulu was walking around the kitchen. She felt strange, her stomach felt really hard. She was wondering if this is what a contraction felt like. Stewart was supposed to get home in two days. She didn't want to have the baby without him. She went to bed and just wished the contractions away. It worked for a few hours, then they started again. She called Adesia and Lilly. They were all circling around the kitchen. "When the contractions are five minutes apart, we have to go to the hospital," said Lilly.

"I know, but Stewart is not going to get here until tomorrow night," said Lulu.

"Sweetheart, nature is not going to wait for Stewart," said Lilly. "We are here for you."

"I know, but I just really wanted Stewart to be here," said Lulu. Lulu couldn't help it. She just started crying. Lilly hugged her. Then Adesia raised her hands in the air, looked up at the ceiling, and started talking to God. "Oh Lord, what is going on? Where are you?

We need you, oh gracious Lord." Then she started singing *Amazing Grace*.

Lilly piped in, "Calm down; everything is going to be fine. We are going to the hospital; your contractions are four minutes apart. Lulu, grab your bag; Adesia, get yourself together."

"I'm talking to God," said Adesia.

"Well, you can talk to him at the hospital. I am sure there are a lot of people there that would like to hear from him," said Lilly.

In 2002, a little girl was born to Lulu and Stewart Wilson. She was their love, hope, and imagination of a world where everyone had a chance, everyone was welcome, and everyone had a voice. It didn't matter what color you were, how rich you were, who you were; what mattered was if you were good, fair, conscientious, and caring. Stewart arrived one day late. He was so sorry to have missed the birth of his daughter. He hoped that Lulu would be able to forgive him. Lulu smiled when he entered the room. She knew his heartache; she understood. She held out her hand. He entered the room, tears in his eyes. He took her hand. "I am so sorry," he said. "I got back as soon as I could."

She saw the pain in his face. "It's Ok, Adesia and Lilly were here. Everything went well. We have a beautiful daughter. I hope you don't mind; I called her America."

"I love her name, and I love you," said Stewart. "You are the beginning and the ending of all I have ever wanted."

The Tragedy

A few years passed. The young couples lived and enjoyed their lives. They had parties with family, they sang and cooked and celebrated life. America was a good baby, and Stewart made the most of the time he had with his daughter and his wife.

It was like any other day. Stewart was scheduled to go up north soon, but first, he drove America to school and Edward to his office. On the way, they had a terrible accident. Edward died instantly, and Stewart saw that America was bleeding from her chin to her eye. They were just across the street from the hospital. He picked her up and started running. It was noon and there were people crowding the street. He yelled for people to let him pass as he ran carrying America. Some people were bothered by his pushing, and others understood. "She has been in an accident!" he said. "I'm sorry, I'm sorry," he continued as he pushed passed people. He arrived at the hospital. Her face was covered in blood. "Help her, please!" he said as he ran in the door.

The man at the entrance said, "Please take a number, and we will get to you soon."

"I am not taking a number!" he said. "I need help now!"

A nurse saw the commotion and told him to follow her. She took him to emergency. She lost a lot of blood. They stitched her up, but she would have a big scar. Stuart was unharmed but was having a hard time understanding what happened. *Oh God, why spare me? Help my daughter and save Edward.*

Lilly was usually a strong person. The giver of strength and optimism, but with the news of Edward, she was crushed. She felt like a balloon that was deflated. She lost the love of her life. She had fallen in love at fourteen. Everyone had said that she was too young, but he stuck by her all these years. He was her rock. The love of her life. Now, he was gone. She felt that he was the reason that she was strong. Without him, she felt she had no strength.

Lulu entered Lilly's apartment. Lilly was cuddled in a ball on the sofa. Lulu just sat next to her and snuggled close.

"I don't want to talk," said Lilly.

"That is Ok, let's watch a movie," said Lulu. She put on *A Series of Unfortunate Events*. "Hey, if those kids can get through that, so can you," said Lulu, knowing that it was not at all helpful. Lilly smiled.

Three months later, Lilly visited Lulu. Lulu could tell something was wrong. "What is the matter? What is bothering you?"

Lilly was agitated and stressed. She let out a sigh. She teared up. "I am pregnant!"

Lulu was stunned. "Oh my god, really?"

"Oh, Lulu, what am I going to do?" asked Lilly.

Lulu thought for a moment. "You are going to have a baby! A little Edward!" said Lulu.

"I can't afford a baby!" said Lily. "I can't hardly do anything. I have trouble getting up in the morning." Lulu hugged her. "I am months back on the rent. I can't stop crying." My life is a mess."

Lulu thought for a moment. "You are going to move in with me and Adesia. We will take care of each other. We will be a family. It is all going to work out."

Adesia, Lulu, and Lilly all moved into Lilly's apartment because it had three bedrooms. They all shared the rent. Stewart was gone for weeks at a time but made good pay.

Lily's New Interest

Lilly took an interest in fortune-telling. She bought a set of Scapini Tarot cards. They were very mysterious-looking. She started memorizing all the meanings of each card. It would take a while. She borrowed books from the library, even though reading was not her thing, so she could learn how to tell fortunes convincingly. She learned how to read a person's posture, palm reading, and how to interpret facial expressions, and she even bought some sparkly purple fabric to put over an old table to create the right ambiance. She called herself Madame Moon Raven. She had business cards made with her name and phone number.

The most useful thing she did in her new career was listening and observing. She started watching the people around her. She would sit quietly and listen to people's conversations. She watched how people would stand, whether they would cross their hands or put their hands on their hips. She watched their every move while listening to what they were saying. She listened to all the gossip, so she could have a hint into people's lives. She wasn't judging anyone; she just wanted to know how people behaved so she could be a successful fortune teller. One day, Lulu and Lilly were shopping at the Salvation Army. Lilly was just following Lulu, not really interested in anything, until she spotted something on a shelf—caught her interest. A crystal ball. "Just what I need," she said.

"What are you going to do with that?" asked Lulu with a smile."

"It is for my new career," said Lilly with excitement and delight.

"Can you divine what I am thinking right now?" said Lulu with a chuckle. "Why do you want to be a psychic?"

After a pause, Lilly said, "Because maybe I could have told Edward to wait a few minutes before leaving for work. Maybe I could have saved his life. Maybe I . . . could be with him right now." Tears welled up in her eyes. "Maybe America would not have her scar, and we would all be happy."

"Sometimes scars make you stronger," said Lulu. "It is not the event that scars you but how you live with it."

Very late that night, Lilly was sitting in the living room in her favorite spot on the sofa. Lulu, America, and Adesia were sleeping. She turned on the little lamp and pulled out the card of the day. Every day, she chose a card to memorize. Today, it was the Queen of Cups. This signified a warm-hearted person. Good friend and mother. A devoted wife and honest, loving, and intelligent person with a gift of vision. Lilly sighed and snuggled under a warm blanket. She thought she saw little lights. She fell asleep on the sofa.

Chapter 13
America

America was a good baby. She was always happy and smiling. Stewart's mother had given America a set of blocks. They had numbers on them. She was mesmerized by the numbers. Lulu showed her the blocks and told her what numbers were on them. She remembered them right away. "This is two, and this is a three," said Lulu.

"Two and three together is five," said America.

Lulu realized that America liked numbers, so she bought other toys that would interest her. America learned to talk and loved math at a very early age. America saw her mother's sudoku puzzle on the table. She solved the puzzle in about five minutes. Lulu gave her a new puzzle. Five minutes later, she had solved it. She bought her an abacus. America was moving the beads at lighting speed whenever Lulu asked her to solve something. How many days in a year? How many minutes in a year? How many Thursdays in a year?

When America was three, she started reading. She read all sorts of stories but loved anything that had to do with math and numbers. She started reading the newspapers. One day at breakfast, she announced to her mother that she wanted to invest in the stock market. "Momma, if I buy this stock in six months, I will have doubled my investment. Can I have an apple?"

Lulu just looked at her. "What?"

"This stock is going to be very valuable in the future, and I really would like an apple right now and maybe some oatmeal. I'm hungry," said America.

Lulu opened a brokerage account for America. Little by little, she invested in what her daughter suggested. Her investment grew and grew." America, this is the money that your grandfather gave me. He wanted me to have a better future. He would have loved and been very proud of you," said Lulu.

Lilly's Struggle

Lilly went to bed very tired. She struggled every day to be optimistic. She knew the people around her were affected by her mood, so she tried to be happy. She did think that someday things would get better. However, they were not better now. She was mad at God for taking Edward. *Take someone else. There are so many mean people that could have been taken. Why not take them? Why take the one good thing she had?* Lily walked to the porch railing. They were on the third floor. She looked down. For a fleeting second, she thought, *It would be simple*, but then the baby started kicking. She remembered that another life was depending on her.

She walked away from the railing. Then her water broke. The baby was coming. Lilly got a weird thought: *I am Delphia, and you are loved.*

Lilly was giving birth on the way to the hospital in a taxi. Adesia was sitting in the front seat of the taxi, talking to God. "Dear God, what are you thinking? We need time to get to the hospital!" Lily was lying in the backseat. This Surprisingly, was not the taxi driver's first birthing rodeo. He had towels and, a seat pad, disinfectant, and a bag of essentials.

Suddenly, the baby just plopped out. Lilly picked her up and held her on her stomach. Lulu was leaning over the front seat. "Look, she is smiling," said Lilly.

"Babies don't really smile," said the taxi driver; "it is just a reflex. It is probably just a burp."

"It's not a burp," said Adesia with indignation. "What do you know? You just keep driving!" Adesia raised her hands in the air. Then she started singing *Amazing Grace*. Lilly and Lulu started laughing.

Chapter 14
Delphia

Delphia was an adorable baby. She was easy and calm unless you turned the television on. Then she cried endlessly. Lilly didn't realize that it was the television that was upsetting her. Once, Delphia was screaming, and Lilly was just exhausted, so she just turned everything off and slumped on the sofa. Delphia stopped crying, and for once, there was silence. Lily took her baby in her arms. She looked at her daughter. "If you want peace, you will get it," she said with a smile.

When Delphia was three years old. She was sitting on the sofa. Lilly was hunting frantically for her keys. "I'm going to be late for work," she said. She started hunting through all of her handbags and coat pockets. She checked everywhere that she thought she could have put her keys. When the clock struck eight, Delphia pulled the keys out of the back of the sofa and held them up for her mother. Delphia smiled, but Lilly was too stressed to notice. She just grabbed the keys and took off; she was going to be late for work.

On her way to work she saw that there was a terrible accident right in front of the building. Six people were injured. It dawned on her, that had she been there earlier, she may have been injured also.

Thanksgiving Visit

When Delphia was seven, Lilly decided to take a trip to see Edward's parents. She took America with her because Lulu could not get away that weekend, and Lilly thought it would be fun for the girls. Edward's parents were delighted to have them over. They really wanted to get to know their granddaughter. They lived in Falmouth, Massachusetts. On their way, Delphia was feeling sick. America was sleeping in the back seat. "Mom, I don't feel good," she said. "Can you stop for a minute?"

Lilly stopped the car. Delphia got out and did the most curious thing. She ran up an embarkment to a school. She ran to the school, only to return not long after. She got back into the car. "I am feeling much better," she said as she sat down.

"Are you sure, sweetie?" asked Lilly.

"Yes, it is the best that I could do."

"What do you mean by that?" asked Lilly

"Well, you can't save everyone, so you save the ones you can," she said in her soft, quiet voice. Delphia laid down on the front seat with her head on her mom's lap. Lilly, not really knowing what Delphia was going through, rubbed her back lovingly the way a mother does.

All of the aunts were coming for Thanksgiving weekend. The house was buzzing with action. Delphia, America, and Lilly were given a room on the second floor. There were two double beds in the room. Delphia was looking out of the window. It overlooked the ocean. It was a quiet rural neighborhood. A dog barked, and she could hear children laughing as they were bicycling down the street. America was taking a nap.

Delphia saw her grandfather pull into the driveway. Right behind him, there was a car with some of her aunts. Everyone was greeting each other with smiles and hugs. When Delphia came down the stairs, all the aunts were surprised. "Oh, my, she looks just like Edward," said Aunt Paxe. "Not a bit like her mother."

"Don't say that! "Said, Bela Flore. "She has her mother's intelligence and strength!"

"You can't see if someone has intelligence and strength," said Paxe.

"Yes, I can!" said great-grandmother Bela Flore.

Lilly came down the stairs. "Calm down, everyone," she said.

Aunt Fiametta started braiding Delphia's long brown hair and gave her a kiss on the top of her head. Despite all the fuss, Delphia was calm. Her grandfather entered the room. Delphia had a sudden vision. She wanted to talk to her grandfather alone, but she would have to wait a while. Just then America came down the stairs. Lilly introduced her. "This is America," she said, "Lulu's daughter."

"Hello, everyone," said America.

"Come here said Aunt Fiametta, and she started braiding America's hair. Just then Aunt Zanobia and Antonella entered the room with trays of food and drink. Aunt Allegra started playing the piano, and Aunt Rosanna started singing. They all enjoyed a wonderful Thanksgiving feast. Delphia and America made a racket on the piano and drank as much cream soda as they could. Everyone went to bed happy and satiated.

The Confrontation

America and Delphia woke up early. They went to see if Delphia's grandfather was up. He was in his office. He was nursing a headache due to the previous evening's celebrations. "Come give Grandpa a hug," said Gerald, Delphia's grandfather. She climbed onto his chair and sat on the side. They had an awkward hug. America took the chair in front of the desk.

"So, how are you today?" he asked Delphia.

"I'm good, it is very nice here. The ocean is beautiful. I could see all the stars last night. Aunt Paxe and Aunt Fiametta are taking us swimming in the ocean this afternoon! We are going to have a picnic on the beach."

"That's nice," said Gerald.

After an awkward silence, Delphia said, "Grandpa, you are thinking of investing in the Starlight Hotels. America and I have discussed it, and we have come to the conclusion that you should not. They are going to be charged with tax evasion and money laundering. You will lose a lot of money," said Delphia.

Gerald looked startled. He chuckled to himself. "How do two little girls know anything?" said Gerald.

"I know you are cheating on grandma," said Delphia.

"And I know that it would cost you dearly," said America.

Gerald got mad. "What do two stupid little girls know? Did your mother put you up to this? Edward would have been so disappointed in you," said Gerald.

Delphia jumped off of the chair. "No, Grandpa, he moved to New York to get away from you! Dad loved me, and he loved my mother," said Delphia.

"That stupid little New Yorker, ha! She was just a pastime. And he would have eventually come to his senses," scoffed Gerald. "And what is this street girl doing here? A black girl in my home! What is this world coming to?"

The next day, the aunts all said goodbye to the girls. They had little gifts to amuse the girls on the car ride back. Gerald was standing at the top of the stairs. Delphia just stared at her grandfather. Just before leaving, she looked at him and stuck out her tongue, something very satisfying when you are young.

"Aren't you going to say goodbye to Grandpa?" asked Lily.

"No," said Delphia.

Delphia Visions

Delphia often had visions, but lately, they were getting more disturbing. Adesia, Lulu, Lilly, and Delphia were all having supper one night. Stewart was working. "What's the matter, Delphia? Aren't you hungry?" asked Lilly.

"No! I can't stop thinking about my visions. They are really scary," she said.

"Delphia. Would it help to talk about it?" asked Lilly.

"Mom, it's terrible. I see the water rising. I see unimaginable storms. I see people being shot. I see people in cages. I see missiles coming." Then she started crying.

"Oh, I am so sorry, sweetheart," said Lilly. It dawned on Lilly that seeing the future was not always a good thing and that it had to be a lot for a child to handle. America was just sitting and listening. Adesia was praying to God quietly.

"What is the point of having visions," asked Delphia, "if we can do nothing about it?"

There was a silence in the room.

"What if we can?" replied America. "What if we can do something about it? These things haven't happened yet. Let's prepare. Maybe the visions are just a warning. Let's get together and do something about it."

That was the night Union fait la force was born. Lulu, America, and Lilly had enough investments to build the building. They hid on the thirteenth floor so they would be safe. To start, they sent out Ben and Bob Booker, twin brothers, to find people with special talents. Everyone laughed when Ben and Bob entered the office with plaid shirts. They still had on dress pants with a belt and shiny shoes. They tucked in the shirts.

"Do you really think you look inconspicuous?" asked Lily with a smile.

"You said blend, so we're blending," said Ben.

"Yeah, I think we look good," said Bob.

"Hey, and I love the watch," said Ben as he held it up. "Can you light it up?"

"That is only for emergencies," said Lulu. "When it lights up, it is a private line between only those who have the watch."

"Ok," said Ben. "We heard of a kid in a small mountain town with an unusual toy, so we are going to check him out. "There was an article in the papers that said that cookies cured people at the hospital," said Bob.

Chapter 15
Catherine Belmont

Catherine was walking on the beach. She was six months pregnant. Her long blond hair was whipping in the wind. She was miserable. She told her parents that she was pregnant and in love. They wanted to get married and raise the baby. Her parents were furious. They lived in Washington, and her father was a senator. They didn't want a scandal. Christian's parents wanted her to get an abortion. Catherine refused. The parents got together and made a plan. They would send Catherine away for a while and give the baby up for adoption. Christian came to see her before she left. He climbed in the window on the third floor into her room. They spent a couple of minutes just holding each other. He felt the baby move. He dropped a few tears and said that he was sorry that he did not have the strength to fight his father. He had two silver rings made with Cand C forever inscribed on the inside with a little heart symbolizing their baby in the middle. Catherine, I will find you someday, and we will be together at last. They had one last kiss, and he left the way he came.

They sent her to an aunt's house who lived in Westport to have the baby. She wanted to stay home, but her father wouldn't hear of it. She had no money and no power to make her own choices. She had to drop out of college.

Her aunt was a cool and aloof woman who thought that Catherine was just a brat. Catherine saw the large stone building. The front door was open, and light was streaming out of the house like a beacon. She slowly approached and looked around. She thought that it looked very welcoming, not like the super modern, efficient, sparse, locked down, and patrolled home she was used to. She called out to see if anyone was home, not sure what she would say if someone answered. Hello, hello she said tentatively. There was no answer. She slowly opened the door. She looked for a bathroom. Then she noticed the light coming from Sofia's apartment.

She peeked in. It looked so cozy. Then she noticed the fridge. Her Aunt thought she needed to be punished for her behavior, so she only fed her once a day. She slowly opened it. There were all sorts of delicious-looking food. She made herself a plate and sat in the big poufy chair. It was getting dark. She put the little light on. She was thinking that if she just could have persuaded her parents, just had a good argument for her case, that she could have changed their minds, she could have made her own decisions, and maybe someone would have taken her side. She fell asleep for a few minutes. She thought she saw lights swirling in the room. *Oh, no, they are coming home!* She ran out of the building, leaving the door open.

Catherine gave birth a month early. Her parents had arranged to have the baby adopted. She only had him for a few minutes. She could not help but feel connected to this child; it was her child. She hung on to him when the nurse came to get the baby; she clung on and turned away. This is my child! She was crying. The couple in the next room could hear her. They were here to adopt the child. The adoptive mother came to the door. The nurse told her to wait in the next room. She came in anyway. She stood next to the bed. She told Catherine that she was blessing them with the greatest gift that a person can give another. I will love and care for your child like he was my own. Then she whispered in her ear that if later in life you want to come to see him, you can. That's enough said Catherine's father. Catherine realized that she had no choice. She made one request. She wanted his first name to be Amell. It was an unusual name, but she liked the meaning of "The power of an eagle." She thought that maybe later in life, it would help to find him. They looked like nice people. She heard that they were farmers.

She was sent back home, but nothing was ever the same again. The first week she was reminded every few hours that she was supposed to be feeding a baby. She felt a great loss. She didn't see people the same way anymore. She needed a change. She didn't want to live with her parents but had no money to move out. She decided to join the red cross. She thought joining the red cross would help people and get her as far away as possible.

Wendy and Richard

Wendy and Richard Scott had been wanting a baby for ten years. Finally, they were able to adopt a son. He was a beautiful baby. They loved him unconditionally. They knew this kid came from someone else with someone else's background. They didn't have any expectations, they just wanted someone to love. They were wheat farmers in Nebraska. They had a nice home in the middle of miles and miles of wheat fields. They thanked God for their blessings.

Amell was very smart and not at all interested in farming. He loved school, books, debating, the thrill of getting better grades than anyone else in the class, and, most of all, winning. He liked to dress neatly. He didn't like to get dirty. He liked baseball because he thought it was more civilized than football. He was not about to let a bunch of heathens tackle him. He knew that when he grew up, he was going to live in a city. His favorite program was *Commander in Chief* and *Law and Order*. He thought video games were a waste of time. When you won the game, there was no reward. He wanted to be a lawyer. This did not make him many friends in Nebraska.

He could not imagine himself driving a big green tractor for hour after hour, up and down the rows. His parents tried to convince him of the beauty and wonder of farming, how vital it was for the survival of the planet. Amell was having none of that. He loved his parents but didn't understand why they seemed to be so content. They generally seemed to think they had the best lives. They would sit on the porch at night after a hard day of work and just rock, listen to country music, and watch the wheat swaying in the wind. Amell was bored out of his mind.

Washington

When Amell was ten, his parents took him to Washington on vacation. Politics did not interest Richard or Wendy, but Amell loved it. He wanted to visit the White House, the Washington

Monument, and the Lincoln Memorial. He knew all the president's names and histories. He was so excited about the trip. It was the first time that Amell had been out of Nebraska. He realized just how large the farms were. Amell leaned forward in the truck and lowered the radio.

"Did you know that President Jefferson invented the swivel chair?" said Amell.

"I did not know that," said his father, smiling.

"And did you know John Quincy Adams used to skinny-dip in the Potomac River?" Then he started giggling and whispering. "A reporter sat on his clothes and refused to leave unless he gave her an interview!"

"Well, Son, that is funny," said Wendy.

He told them little tidbits of history for a couple of hours. Finally, he fell asleep, leaning on his mother. Richard said, "We certainly will be well-educated by the time we get to Washington!" Wendy gave him a knowing smile.

They were visiting the Lincoln Memorial when Amell was knocked over by a man with a briefcase that was going down the steps with a group of people. The man was tall and dressed like a lawyer. Amell was just getting up when the man noticed. He put his briefcase down. "Are you Ok, Son?" asked the man with the briefcase. "I'm so sorry I didn't see you there. What's your name?"

"Amell," he said with a smile.

"Here," he reached in his pocket and handed Amell a shiny new 2012 American Silver Eagle.

"Thanks, sir," he said with a big smile.

"Good afternoon," he said while tipping his hat.

Wendy and Richard realized that their son would never be a farmer. They put money aside to send him to college. They did not always understand their son, but they believed that everyone was their own person and had their own ambitions. Richard never wanted to be anything but a farmer. Wendy was very happy to be a farmer's wife. They knew their son was different. They wanted their son to go after his own dreams, not theirs.

Chapter 16
The Crofts

Charlotte always wanted to be a mother. She wanted a large family. She married her high school sweetheart. They had four children. Two boys, Thomas and Bruno, and twin girls, Carly and Caren. She was passing the vacuum one day and decided that four children were enough. She had a little heartburn, so she took a rest. They had a small home in Buzzards Bay, Massachusetts. She liked to think it was full of love.

Charlotte liked to read. When the kids got older, George and Charlotte bought a small sofa and another television to put in their bedroom because there was always so many of her children's friends in the living room. This worked for a while. Her husband, George, liked to watch the news and go to bed.

Charlotte was sitting in her bed one night and thinking to herself. *I need my own place to read. A little piece of heaven, right now, before I die.* She realized that she was being a little dramatic. She got up and paced around the small house. Her husband was sleeping in the bedroom, so that was not an option. The kids were in the living room playing Nintendo, the girls were doing their homework with a couple of friends in the kitchen . . . then she saw the closet. Ah, the closet. She opened the door to the closet. Stuff was falling out. *That's Ok*, she thought. She got some garbage bags and returned to the closet. Anything that was not necessary to their existence she put in the bags that were destined for the Salvation Army. The rest she relocated, meaning she dumped it into the kid's rooms. This was her space, her room, her little magical reading room.

She went shopping and bought a very comfortable flowered chair. She bought a cute little lamp at the Salvation Army. She bought some light blue and white paint. She painted the closet blue with a cloud-effect ceiling. Then she made a little shelf for the lamp and placed bookshelves from floor to ceiling on the wall in front of the chair. Now, she had her own little reading space. She hung a sign on the door like in a hotel, "Do Not Disturb."

Her heartburn wasn't going away. She made a doctor's appointment. "Charlotte, you are perfectly healthy, you are just pregnant!" She was disappointed for a few minutes, but she got over it. *One last child.*

The Crofts had just finished supper. There were dishes and, schoolbags and toys everywhere. She looked around the room. What a mess. The kids were watching *Marry Poppins*. She went to her little room. She sat down and was thinking, *Wouldn't it be nice to be able to move things around like Mary Poppins all while sitting in my chair.* She made a few movements with her hand before falling asleep for just a few seconds in her special room. The lights were swirling around.

Zander

Alexander was born in a maze of activity. Charlotte had her mother come help the kids. Time passed but one thing held true. They all loved Zander. They shortened his name, and the nickname stuck. He was like a new toy. He was a super nice child. He was very curious and laughed easily. He loved his pacifier. He watched his siblings with glee. One night, they put him to bed. He slept in a crib in the same room with his brothers, Thomas and Bruno. They were both sleeping. Zander dropped his pacifier on the floor. He looked at the pacifier, he pointed at it, and it lifted off the floor. He pointed it over the sides of the crib and into his hands. Zander realized that he could move things with his fingers.

His brothers often played with marbles. He found them fascinating. He would make them follow him wherever he went. Charlotte was very busy with the family; she didn't notice anything strange. With all the commotion of five children, you tend not to notice the little things. Every time she had a chance; she would find peace in her little room. The kids would joke with their friends. "Where's your mom?"

"Oh, she's in the closet again."

Life went on, and Zander grew up. His fifth birthday was coming up. He was sitting at the kitchen table coloring. He was turning the pages of a coloring book. He wasn't actually touching the book; he was flipping through the book to find just the right page.

Charlotte felt that she wanted to do something special for him. She asked him what he would like. He said he wanted a magician's coat and hat, a small folding table, a black tablecloth, and a wand. He had never asked for anything, so she did her best to make his wish come true. "What do you want that for?" she asked.

"I am going to be a magician," he said with confidence. She pulled out the old sewing machine and sewed him a little purple jacket with a shiny, black satin collar. She went to a costume store and bought him a black magician's hat and wand. Then she bought a small table and had George shorten the legs. She bought some purple and black striped tablecloths. She baked a cake, and they all had a little party. She gave him his gift. "Now you can be a magician," she said with a smile and a kiss.

Zander set everything up in his room. He started to practice a little show. Finally, he was ready. Bruno and Thomas brought some blankets to put on the grass. Zander set up his table under a large tree, in his front yard. Bruno set up a cassette player nearby for music. "Ladies and Gentlemen!" He took a bow. He set down a deck of playing cards. Bruno started the music. It was a song from *Aladdin* ("Friend Like Me").

Zander started waving the wand over the cards, and one by one, they got up and started dancing to the music. They made a circle on the table, then they started jumping and flipping. Everyone was amazed. People who were walking by stopped to see the show. For a finale, he made the cards swirl in a tornado-like effect.

"Wow!" said his mom, "you can't see any wires or string! Good job."

Thomas held out the hat after the show and people threw change into the hat. "Look, Zander, you made twenty-five dollars and seventy-five cents," said Bruno.

Zander smiled that big bright smile.

Family Vacation

That summer, there was a free concert in the park in Boston. Charlotte and George decided to have a small vacation with all the kids. They would go to the beach, then go to the park and watch the concert. They would stay at the Holiday Inn so the kids could swim in the pool, and there was a free breakfast in the morning. Everyone was very excited. Zander packed his magic kit. George was packing the suitcases in the car.

"Zander, you can't bring a table!"

"Oh, please Dad, unscrew the legs from the top. Then it will fit in. Please, please please!"

George relented, and he smiled at his son, "Ok, I guess I can fit it in."

The family all swam in the ocean, then went to the park. Zander set up his table. He put on the tablecloth. Then he pulled his jacket and hat out of a duffel bag and put it on. He set down a deck of cards. He performed his show. He made one hundred and ninety-five dollars. He gave the money to his dad to help with the trip's expenses.

"Zander, this is yours. You earned it," said his dad.

"I don't need it right now, and someday when I am the great and magical Zander," he said, writing his name in the sky, "then I will have all the money I need." He hugged his father.

Typical Zander Style

It was a beautiful autumn day, and Zander was making all the leaves follow him in the shape of a dragon as he walked down the street. Some guy got out of a black SUV and took a picture, then he quickly sped away. Zander got a weird feeling but just brushed it off. He turned the dragon into a tornado, then let it fall slowly back down to the ground. He continued to school.

Zander was very personable, so everyone liked him. He had unruly hair in a cool sort of way. He was very self-confident; he knew what he wanted and what he didn't want. He didn't feel like he had to please anyone, but he liked to please the people he liked. He did little tricks to please his friends. For example, the girl next to him in class one day was missing a pencil. Suddenly, one just flew through the air, doing a few flips before landing on her desk.

Zander sat next to Sunny at lunchtime. Sunny was in a wheelchair. He was hit by a drunk driver when he was young. He didn't remember any of it. His parents came from Mexico. They were able to immigrate to the United States because Sonny's father was a scientist. His father lamented once that he could create a vaccine that could cure millions, but he could not help his son.

"Hey Sunny, how is it going?" asked Zander.

Sunny looked at him and smiled.

Zander placed his tray on the table. "What would you like to eat? I will get it for you," said Zander.

"I would like the veal parmesan and an ice cream sandwich, please." He gave Zander some money for lunch.

Zander went and got Sunny the veal parmesan. While he was gone to get the food, Bruce Hilton sat down next to Sunny. "What are you doing, stupid Sunny?"

"Go away," said Sunny.

"Who gave you that stupid name?" asked Bruce.

"My mother and, leave me alone."

"Or what?" taunted Bruce. "Why don't you roll yourself back to Mexico?" he said with a menacing tone.

Sunny was trying to think of something to say. People around him were starting to stare at him. He was embarrassed. Suddenly, fruit salad started flying in the air and landing on Bruce! First just a grape, then a peach slice, then a piece of pineapple, then a cherry, then a mix of all of them. Sunny started laughing, and everyone else started laughing except Bruce.

"Hey, it is a little messy here," said Zander, "let's move over." The two boys took a seat farther down the table. Everyone knew from then on not to bug Zander and Sunny. The two boys became best friends.

Zander decided to join the ping-pong club. Sunny came to watch. It took a while for Zander to get the flow of the game. Then he noticed that he could control the ping-pong ball with his mind. He started to win. It was great fun. Zander was a natural showman. He swung this way and that way and made impossible shots. He beat everyone in the room.

For the final game, the winner would get a prize. Sunny was in the audience. He motioned to Zander that he wanted to talk to him. Zander went to talk to his friend. Something changed in his demeanor after that. Zander lost the match and the championship.

"Are you Ok?" asked Sunny.

"Yes. And you are right, it isn't fair for me to use my mind skills in a competition. ," said Zander.

Zander changed his focus to his new act. He bought five colorful bowling balls. Then he started to practice. He was piling them one onto another and slowly having them move in circles when suddenly his brother Thomas walked into the small bedroom. Zander was startled, and one ball went through his bedroom window. "Oh crap," said Zander. Then all the balls fell, and one hit his foot. "Ouch!"

"I really need a better place to practice," said Zander. He realized that he could move larger objects, but he really had to concentrate.

The Robbery

One day, soon after that event, Zander and Sunny were going to watch a basketball game. They stopped at a corner store to buy snacks. Sunny was perusing the chip aisle when someone came in. He had a big coat on. He leaned next to the counter. Zander could not hear what he was saying but he saw the top of the gun in his pocket. He used his gift to lift the gun out of the pocket and threw it on the floor. The would-be robber was startled. Then he saw the gun on the floor. He bent down to pick it up, but the gun skidded farther down the aisle. He thought that he may have kicked it. So, he ran after it. It kept sliding down the aisle. The storekeeper called the police. The gunman was still running after the gun when the police arrived. Zander and Sunny went home without a word.

They told their story while sitting on the counters of the little Croft home and eating apple pie. Wendy Croft was known for her apple pie. The police asked for the store video, but it had mysteriously disappeared. The next day, there was an article in the newspaper about a butterfingers robbery. The guy with the gun complained that the gun was possessed. Everyone laughed.

The New Act

When Zander was twelve, he entered a talent contest. He worked on his act for about two months. His mother sewed him a new costume. It was a black and white tuxedo. The whole family was in the audience.

The stage went dark. Then a light shone on the floor, making a circle. In the circle, there were two chicken feet with long legs. Suddenly, they sprung to life. They were standing and stretching. Then another small light shone on a small cannon on a table. Zander walked on stage to some applaud. He took a bow. Then he lit the small cannon, and with exaggerated motions, plugged his ears. "Poof!" out of the cannon came a ball of pink feathers. The pink feathers slowly fell to the ground. Zander waved his wand, and the feathers formed a big pink bird. He took a beak and eyes out of his pocket and placed them on the bird. The big pink bird fluttered her eyes at him. There was a chuckle from the audience.

Then the music started playing, and Zander and the big bird started dancing around. No one could figure out how he was doing it. They waltzed, jitterbugged, and discoed. Then when the music stopped, Zander put the beak and the eyes back in his pocket. He waved the wand; the pink feathers fell to the floor. Zander took a bow and slowly walked off stage. The chicken feet followed him out.

Chapter 17
Mia and Jun-Ha Sung

Mia Sung and her husband, Jun-Ha Sung, lived in the little town of Bar Harbor, Maine. They had a small family business selling mementos to tourists. They had immigrated from Korea. They felt a bit out of place in Maine, but some of the neighbors had been welcoming. Mia didn't want to sell just postcards and T-shirts, so she made an effort to sell products from the artisans in the area. This endeared her to the locals in the small town. Her mother lived with them. She was elderly and had Alzheimer's. Every day, her mother would lose a few more memories.

Mia was expecting her first child. They had a cozy apartment over their shop that overlooked the ocean. She was watching her mother wandering around the apartment, trying to remember what she was looking for. Mia sat back in the chair and wished there was a cure for her mother's disease. She was sure that Mother Nature had a cure for every disease on earth, but the trick was to find it. As it was getting dark, she turned on a little lamp she had bought at a secondhand store. She saw lights dancing in the room. She thought it was the reflection of the sun on the water.

Penelope

When Mia had the baby, Mia was very sick. She almost died. The doctor told her it would be better not to have any more children. Mia was very disappointed. They named the little girl Penelope.

Penelope loved plants. Mia had to put the plants up high so Penelope would not eat them. When they took walks, Penelope would pick up plants and stick them in her pockets, along with stones and small bugs. Jung-Ha thought it was both strange and funny. Penelope would enter the house with her pockets full and try to pretend that nothing was suspicious.

"What is in your pockets?" asked Mia.

"Nothing," said Penelope, looking at the ceiling. She would go to her room, where she had a collection of jars on a shelf and on the windowsill. She had a small peg board that she would hang the bugs to dry them out. She borrowed her mother's mortar and pestle.

The Pills

Slowly, the grandmother seemed to be getting better. She started reading again, something she hadn't done in a long time.

"Mom, when were you born?" asked Mia.

"February 23, 1941. Why do you ask," she said in Korean.

Mia thought that she was having a reprise from the illness. Then one morning, Mia saw Penelope giving some pills to the grandmother. "Oh my God, what are you doing?" asked Mia. She ran to the grandmother and tried to stick her finger in her mouth like you would a child, to remove the pills. The grandmother gently grabbed her hands.

"I want the pills," she said.

"What are these pills?" she asked.

"I am making grandma remember things," said Penelope. I call them Remember me pills.

"How long have you been giving her the pills? asked Mia.

"Three weeks," said Penelope.

After Mia sat down for a few moments, she said. "Show me how you do it."

Penelope went to her room and showed Mia a paste that she had made in the mortar and pestle. "I roll these into pills and dry them out. Mom, I know what I am doing. Grandma is getting better. Mother nature is helping me."

Mia remembered the thought she had a while back about Mother Nature and her mother. She believed in her daughter.

Business Venture

"Mom, I want to sell my pills," said Penelope.

"What? How many do you have?" she asked.

"Right now, about five kinds, but if you would drive me a little farther out of town, I could collect more specimens. I have Big Hair, Fart Attack, Smart Pills, Giggle Pills, and Remember Me. Some of them are more serious, and some are funny. Mom, let's try the Big Hair together!"

Mia was skeptical but went along with it. She giggled and took the pills with her daughter. The next morning, Jun-Ha was laughing when his wife and daughter had the same hair style at the breakfast table, straight up! Mia and her daughter looked at each other.

"Penelope, we need nice bottles and good mysterious labels and a nice rack to sell them on. Then you can sell them here and to other stores."

Penelope hugged her mom.

"Hey, don't forget me," said the grandmother.

Jun-Ha built the racks, Mia ordered the bottles and designed the labels, Penelope made the pills and potions, and Grandma put the labels on the bottles. It was a family effort.

New Friend

One day, Mia took Penelope and went on a plant scavenger hunt. They drove all over the countryside, with Penelope getting out of the car every few miles to collect specimens. She would run in the fields and by the ponds. She placed all her findings in bottles and Ziplock bags. Mia was very patient.

Mia didn't quite understand her daughter, but she believed in her. They stayed at a Holiday Inn. In the morning, they went for the continental breakfast. Penelope was eating scrambled eggs and peach yogurt when she noticed a small boy using an inhaler. He looked sickly. Later, she saw him at the pool.

"Hi, I am Penelope, what is your name?"

"I'm Nathan," he said. "Hey, do you want to race?" she asked him.

He looked at her for a moment. "I can't," he said, "but I would really like to."

Penelope knew what to do. She went to the hotel kitchen and asked for a spoon, bowl, knife, mortar and pestle, and cornstarch. They thought she was cute, so they obliged her. She brought the items back to the hotel room.

"Mom, do you have matches?" That night, Penelope mixed things, cooked, crushed, and mushed, and blended the things she had found that day.

Mia saw little blue sparks coming out of the mortar and pestle. "Make sure you don't set off the fire alarm," said her mother while dozing off.

It took her all night, but she made him pills. She went to Nathan's door to give them to him. A man opened the door. "Who are you?" asked the man.

"I have something for Nathan. We met yesterday at the pool." She showed him the pills.

"What, are you crazy? I am not giving my son anything from you. Go back to China!" He slammed the door in her face.

She was hurt but didn't quite understand the insult. She would have loved to visit China someday, but first she wanted to visit Korea, where her parents were born. She asked the front desk for

Nathan's address. They thought she had a crush on him, so they gave her the address. Penelope decided that she would just send him the pills and leave the rest up to chance.

I Want a Sister

After Penelope and her mom returned from their trip, they settled onto the couch next to each other. Penelope said, "Mom, why don't I have any sisters?"

"Well, the doctor says that I shouldn't have any more children. It would be a big risk."

"Mom, I have a pill for that," said Penelope.

Mia smiled. "In any case, I doubt that I could even get pregnant," said Mia.

"Mom, I want a sister. Look, just take this beautiful pink pill. I sweetened it with sugar—not good for you but it tastes infinitely better."

In a moment of bonding, she took the pill.

Mia was looking over the new racks that Jun-Ha had built. They had a place for the bottles and the pills. The labels that her mother designed were mysterious and beautiful. They had Penelope's potions on the front. Mia was putting any profits toward Penelope's education. Penelope wanted to be a botanist. Mia figured that her daughter had a head start.

They started selling the pills in their store and sold some to other stores. They got to be very popular. Someone even offered to pay them for the recipes. They said no, of course. Soon after the shop was broken into, some of the recipes were stolen but most of them were not written down. It was all in Penelope's imagination. Penelope noticed the black SUV speeding away.

Chapter 18
Matoaka and Douglass

Matoaka lived on an Indian reservation. She lived alone with her mother. Her father had left many years ago. Her one desire was to go to college. She loved anything to do with the weather. Storms excited her, and warm winds intrigued her, she wanted to understand what caused a storm. She wanted to be a meteorologist.

Her first job was at a department store. She was determined to save money to go to get an education. She only did free activities. She helped people, took care of her mother and her mother's friends, and cooked and cleaned. She had a simple life, but she had a goal. Finally, she saved enough to go to college. Her mother and her mother's friends had a little party for her. They gave her gifts and wished her luck on her journey. Her mother was very proud of her daughter. She bought her a compass.

"This is so you can always find your way home," she said with love in her voice. Matoaka left with three changes of clothes and what she had saved up in the bank. She was in her last year of college when she met Douglass. He was six feet four, and she was five feet tall. He was blond with a receding hairline, and she had long brown hair. They made a very odd-looking couple. He was studying to be an astronomer.

He noticed that she went to eat her lunch every day in the park across from the college. She always brought a bagged lunch. One day, he bought lunch in the cafeteria and brought it to the park. He was doubting his choice when he realized that soup was hard to carry. He had spilled most of it by the time he tried to nonchalantly put down the tray. Matoaka laughed.

"For a big guy, it looks like you are not going to eat much today."

He looked at his bowl. "Yeah, I think you are right." He smiled. He was thinking that it didn't matter. "So, what are you studying today?" he asked.

"I am learning about weather patterns and how to predict them."

"Oh, that sounds a little tedious," he said.

"Oh no, it is fascinating!" she said. There was an awkward silence.

"There is going to be a meteorite shower tomorrow. Would you like to see it," he coughed a little, "with me?"

She looked at him, "Yes, I would, but this better not be some ploy to get me to do something that I don't want to do."

He understood. He smiled. "It's a date then. I will pick you up in my hunk a junk, and we will find a place to watch the stars collide!"

She smiled.

Douglass showed up in a rusty, beat-up pickup truck. She tried to open the door. "Oh, wait, there is a trick to that," he said. He bounded out of the truck then fiddled with the handle until it finally opened. Douglass looked very relieved. "My lady," he said with a smile.

She climbed in. "Wow, there is a lot of stuff in this truck," she said.

He looked around. "Yeah, I guess so." He felt a little embarrassed. *Why didn't I think to clean up before now?* he was thinking.

She pushed over a few bags of fast food and, an old sweater, some tools, big rubber waders, and a fishing box. "You know, if the world ended right now, we could probably survive with what is in the truck," she said with a smirk.

"Ok, so I suppose that is a good thing," he said. She laughed.

They drove to the top of a hill. The little mountain rose above the desert. It was called Little Rock Mountain. It was the perfect place to stargaze. Douglass spread out a quilt for a picnic.

"So, no soup?" asked Matoaka. Douglass smiled.

"Nope, lesson learned," he said. He had sandwiches, chips, grapes, and gingerale. It was a beautiful starry night. They had their picnic and watched the stars fly by. At that moment, he knew he could not live his life without her. This was not a fleeting thing. As they were watching the stars, he gently leaned over and kissed her.

After they both graduated, they married at city hall. Matoaka's mother could not travel to California for the wedding. She sent a little lamp as a gift. Matoaka sent her mother a phone so they could keep in touch. They bought the little mountain where they had first fallen in love and had seen the stars flying across the sky, where everything was possible. They bought a camper and lived in it while they were building a home.

They had a diviner come to find water. The old man used a divining rod. He was walking back and forth on the property. Suddenly, the branch was pulling down. "This is the place," he said with assurance. They chose the place to build the house, the well, and plant a garden. "I am not sure how long you will have water," said the deveiner, "but you should be good for a while."

When they finished the house, they decided to start a family. Matoaka was talking to her mother late one night. The little lamp filled the room with a soft glow. Matoaka's mother was talking about her great aunt who was rumored to be able to control the weather. "That would be great in California," said Matoaka. "the weather is usually nice here but sometimes it is so dry that the fires start, and the Santa Ana winds blow the flames. Then sometimes it rains so hard it floods certain areas. It would be great to control it," she said with a big yawn.

"Oh, it is getting late," said her mother, "you should get some sleep. Good night, sweetheart, love you."

"Love you, too, Mom." With that, she hung up the phone. She fell asleep on the sofa with little lights dancing in the room.

Shabina

Douglas and Matoaka had a little girl. They called her Shabina. It meant "the eye of the storm." Matoaka liked it because she thought that it represented the calm in the midst of calamity. When Shabina was three years old, the well dried up. They hired another diviner to find water, but he could not find any. "What are we going to do without water?" asked Matoaka.

"I don't know," said Douglas.

Shabina climbed onto her mother. That night, it started raining; well, not just raining, but pouring. It was like a spigot just opened in the sky, and the deluge came down. The well started working again. Matoaka's garden was flourishing. She sold the beautiful produce and flowers in town. It rained every night like clockwork. One night, Matoaka and Douglass were having supper with Shabina.

"Oh, I really like this Shepherd's pie," said Douglass.

"I am glad you like it," said Matoaka. "Douglass, the aphids are eating all of my roses. What do you think we can do about it?"

"I don't know, I will check at the hardware store and see if they have something for that."

The next day, all the aphids had died. They were scattered on the ground under the rose bushes. Bugs to dust.

The Bath

"Shabina, it is time for your bath," said Matoaka.

"I want to wash outside," said Shabina. "I want to wash in the rain."

"It's not raining," said Matoaka.

"It will be," said Shabina. She got a bar of soap, a facecloth, and a towel. She went outside, and it started pouring. Shabina started singing, "Rub a dub dub, three men in a tub," and was washing with the rain and the soap. When she was done, she entered the house. "Oh, that was so refreshing," she said.

"Well, she does have good timing," said Douglass, with a smile.

The Fire

The tumbleweeds and brush had been growing for a while. The earth was getting very dry. It still rained every day on Little Rock Mountain, but the desert around them was drying up. Then the fires started. Lightning struck, and the dry growth started burning. There were huge fires heading for the lush garden on Little Rock. Matoaka and Douglass were watching the fires approach the little farm.

"Do you think we should evacuate," asked Shabina.

"We might have to if the fire gets too close," said Douglass.

Shabina came beside them. She waved her hand to the ground around them. "Goodnight, Mom and Dad. Don't worry." Then she went to bed.

Matoaka and Douglass stayed up and watched the fires, and surely enough, as the fires approached the line that Shabina had drawn, they just died out.

Shabina's Birthday

Matoaka wanted to make a little birthday party for Shabina. She was going to start school. She didn't know who to invite. She sent a ticket to her mother so she could come to spend a week with them. She missed her mother; it had been too long since she had seen her. When she arrived, she realized that her mother didn't look the same. She looked older. She didn't move as fast as she had remembered. However, she still had the quick wit and intelligence that she was used to.

Matoaka's mother was sitting on the porch and watching Shabina playing in the yard. Shabina was wearing a little polka dot dress and had a crown of monarch butterflies on her head. Their wings fluttering and shinning in the sunlight. She had a little yellow watering can in her hands. She was passing the watering can over the flowers, but the water was not coming out of the can but from the sky. Shabina saw her grandmother and smiled. Just then Matoaka came out on the porch with a tray of tall glasses of iced tea. She sat down next to her mother.

"You know that your daughter is a weather spirit," said Matoaka's mother.

"What does that mean?" said Matoaka.

"It means she can control the weather, insects, and fire."

"No one can do that," said Matoaka with a smile.

"In time, you will see," said her mother.

Matoaka called Shabina over, and they drank their tea on the porch. After a while, Matoaka went back into the house to finish some paperwork. "Grandma, can I fly the new kite you bought me yesterday for my birthday?" asked Shabina.

"Sure, go get it, and I will help you."

Shabina bounded into the house and came back a few minutes later with a large kite that had a picture of a dragonfly on it. They assembled it together. Shabina handed the spool of string to her grandmother and ran off into the yard. She threw the kite into the air and pointed at the kite as it rose higher and higher. The wind made the kite dive and flutter in the air. Shabina looked up with delight. "Watch this, Grandma," said Shabina as the kite flew down to the porch, then made two loop de loops in the air and flew over the flower garden. Shabina gave her grandma a hug. "Thank you, Grandma; I love my kite, but what is the string for?"

Shabina's grandma smiled and said, "Some people need string."

Shabina skipped off into the garden followed by a parade of butterflies and a kite.

Matoaka and Shabina went shopping for school clothes. She had a list of items that the school wanted the parents to provide. Shabina was excited about all the crayons and, the purple school bag and lunchbox. Matoaka bought a cute yellow raincoat with daisies all over it and yellow rubber boots. "What is that for? asked Shabina.

"That is a raincoat to keep you dry when you go to school in the rain."

"Oh, what fun! I will wear it tomorrow."

"They are not forecasting rain tomorrow," said Matoaka.

Shabina smiled. The next morning, it was raining buckets. "Good thing we bought the raincoat," said Shabina with a smile.

The Park

One summer during a vacation, Matoaka and Douglass decided to visit Matoaka's mother in Massachusetts. They would make a road trip out of it. They rented a van and set out on their journey. Her mother lived on a reservation. Shabina liked meeting her relatives. They took a day trip to Plymouth Plantation and visited the Mayflower. Shabina really liked visiting the old replica ship. Then they went to Boston for a concert in the park. It rained all the way to Boston. "Maybe we should stop and buy some umbrellas," said Douglass.

"It isn't going to be raining in the park," piped in Shabina. Surely enough, once they got into the park, the clouds parted, and it stopped raining.

Matoaka's mother smiled, "I'm telling you, she is a weather spirit." They watched A magician called Zander perform a fascinating show with cards. Douglass watched intently trying to figure out how the young boy could do those tricks. He left a nice tip.

When Shabina was twelve, she went to spend the summer at her grandmother's. She was gone for two months. While she was gone, the garden dried up. The well stopped working. When she arrived,

Douglass was putting new tires on the camper. Matoaka had already packed. They were going to find a new place to live. Shabina was disappointed, but her parents were more philosophical. "Nothing is permanent," said Matoaka. "Mother nature sighs and yawns, her arms rippling the earth, moving mountains and seas. She changes her dress and then settles down to sleep another thousand years, or until she is awakened by stains and spills and holes on her clothing."

Chapter 19
Jayr's New Friend

When Jayr was nine, Sofia and James decided to take a little holiday in New York City to visit relatives. They needed a break from the restaurant. She had some reliable employees, and everything was going well. They were going to visit Sofia's aunt, who had a bookstore and coffee shop. She sold new and used books, coffee, and various pastries. She also lived above the store. Jayr loved the little shop. It had shelves on every wall that was available, from floor to ceiling.

Jayr would get up in the morning and choose a book from the packed shelves, and his aunt would make him a hot chocolate. He loved the smell of coffee and the quiet murmur of the readers. There was a patchwork sofa in one corner and a couple of small round tables with chairs overlooking the street. Two large double-sided bookcases filled the back of the shop, and on the left side, there was a small counter with a coffee machine and fresh baked goods. He spent the day reading and watching the various customers come and go.

He noticed a girl who came in every day. She was reading a book about the stock market. She was an African American with corn rows and light brown skin. She looked like she had just popped out of a Gap commercial. She had a scar on her face that went from the corner of her mouth to her ear. She seemed to be very self-conscious about it. She kept trying to cover the scar with her hair. "Hi, I'm Jayr," he said. The girl just looked at him. "What are you reading?" he asked.

She hesitated, then she said, "The stock market."

"Why are you reading that?" he asked honestly.

"I love numbers," she said. Then she smiled a shy smile and covered her cheek. She was used to being bullied but didn't get that feeling from him.

"What's your name?" he asked.

"America," she said.

"What happened to your cheek?" he asked. "Can I touch it?"

"No!" she said, and then she went to sit on the sofa across the room. He just sat in his chair and started to read. He kept glancing at her. When she looked at him, he would make a face. She pretended not to notice. Then he took out a bag of M&Ms from his pocket. He was tossing them in the air and catching them with his mouth. Then he suddenly threw one to her. She caught it and smiled before putting her head back in the book. He was reading ghost stories. They sat across from each other for a few hours. Then Jayr approached her again. "I can help you," said Jayr, "but you have to trust me."

Something in the soft, quiet, gentle way he said it, made her believe him. She was still young enough to believe in miracles. He very gently touched her cheek, running his hand from the corner of her mouth to her ear. She felt a tingling sensation.

Jayr smiled at her. "I am tired now; I have to sleep. Go look in the mirror." Then he curled up on the sofa.

America went to the bathroom. She stood on her toes to look in the mirror. She couldn't believe it; the scar was gone! She touched her face and smiled a big smile. On the way out, she left a note for Jayr. He was still fast asleep on the sofa. She tucked it carefully in his hand and ran home to see her mother. Sofia and Jayr's aunt found Jayr sleeping on the sofa. Sofia said, "He sleeps a lot, but the doctor said that he is very healthy."

"He certainly is a good-looking boy," said his aunt, "and he has a gentleness about him. He acts much older than his age." When Jayr woke up, he found the note in his hand. "Please meet me here at 8:00 tomorrow morning. I want to thank you for helping me, America."

The next morning, America came in with a big smile and a swing in her step. They sat at the little table overlooking the street. Jayr's aunt Betty brought them both hot chocolate and freshly baked blueberry muffins. America pulled out an envelope. In it, there was a thousand dollars. "Listen, if you do what I tell you, in two years, you will be rich enough to sleep all day," she said with a smile. "I want you to do two things. First, have your mother open a brokerage account. Then I want you to buy a subscription to *The New York*

Times. Check in the 'Personals' every week, on Monday. Check under 'Dear Monsieur Largent' and follow the instructions. Do you understand?" asked America.

"Sure," said Jayr.

"How did you do it?" America asked Jayr.

He smiled. "I don't know how I do it, but I can heal people. I have always been able to, but I have to sleep after. It is as though it drains all my energy, and I have to sleep to get it back."

"Do your parents know?" she asked.

"I don't think so. It isn't always as obvious as it was for you. Your scar was visible; often the people I heal don't know I healed them. I don't really want people to know. I don't want to be some kind of freak or have my gift be an obligation. I cannot cure everyone, so I want to leave it to chance."

"Ok, your secret is safe with me," said America."

"Where did you get a thousand dollars?" asked Jayr.

"Do you see that skyscraper over there? Those are condos. I live on the thirteenth floor with my mother. That is our building. Would you like to see it?"

"Sure, that would be great," said Jayr.

"Ok, I will let my aunt know that we are coming," said America.

Union fait la force

America and Jayr went to the very tall building. There was a doorman who knew America. "Good morning," she said, smiling as the doorman opened the door. "Thank you," she said. Jayr and America entered into the elevator.

"So what floor are we going to?" asked Jayr.

"The thirteenth," she said.

"There is no thirteenth. It skips from twelve to fourteen," said Jayr.

"Try pushing one and three at the same time," said America.

Jayr followed her instructions. Sure, enough they arrived at the thirteenth floor, and the doors opened. There was a hallway and another door with a large brass Letter U with two brass stars in it.

What does that stand for?" asked Jayr.

It stands for Union fait la force. What does that mean? Is it French?

Yes, it means when you stand together, it makes you stronger. What are the stars for? He asked. They represent our members.

She pushed on the *U*, it clicked down and lit up. Then the door opened to an office. They walked through the office. Then there was a bookcase. America moved a book, and suddenly, the bookcase moved and revealed a door. It led to an apartment. America walked through. "Adesia, I am home, I have a visitor," said America.

"Oh, America, you should not bring strangers here," said Adesia.

"He is not a stranger," said America, "he is the healer that I was telling you about."

"I think God was the healer," said Adesia."

"Yes, but he heals through Jayr," said America.

"Well, it is very nice to meet you, young man," said Adesia. She gave him a big hug. She looked at him in his eyes. "Thank you, son, from the bottom of my heart."

"No singing," said America with a smile. "Where is Mom?"

"She is at the soup kitchen. Adesia and Lulu had opened a soup kitchen to help the people in the neighborhood. They all took turns helping and cooking. They felt very blessed to have the chance to give back. America had made it possible to have enough money for all of them to have a good life.

"Who were the people in the office that we walked through?" asked Jayr.

It is a foundation that my mother and her friend Lilly and daughter, Delphia, and I have started. It is a nonprofit whose goal is to find conscientious and talented people who are interested in working together to make the world a better place for everyone. America showed Jayr her watch. When the watch lights up it means something has happened and people need our help. Just then Delphia walked into the office.

"Hey Del, this is Jayr, the guy I was talking to you about."

"Hey," said Jayr. Delphia had the same watch on. "So, Can I join your club?" asked Jayr.

"No, you have to be eighteen. We have the watches, but they don't work yet. Right now, we are just looking for people for our group."

"Can anyone join?" asked Jayr.

"Yes, anyone who wants to devote themselves to helping others. All for one and one for all. However, this is not for everyone. You will never be super rich or powerful. We all work together; we share what we have. We depend on everyone's talents for our success. The Union is not about money and power, though we do have money and power. We have a list of people that we are keeping an eye on. We will certainly put you on the list!"

Chapter 20
Daniel's Secret

Daniel was sitting in the big, comfy chair reading a Sherlock Holmes mystery. He heard someone knocking on the door. He was surprised to see that it was his mother. "Mom, it is so nice to see you," he said, and gave her a hug. She smiled at him and hugged him back.

"Is there somewhere we can talk?" she asked.

"We can talk here," he said, "we are alone except for Harold who is working in his shop." They sat down on the sofa. "What's new? How is Dad?" said Daniel.

She looked at him with empathy. "I'm sorry, Son, he died last night. He had a heart attack and died in his sleep."

Daniel slumped onto the sofa. "Oh," he said, running his hands through his hair.

She gently took his hand. "Despite everything, you know he loved you."

He sat still for a few moments. "No, I don't know that" he said with tears and anger. "He threw me out of the house with nothing. He didn't care about me, and I am not sure you did either. Why did you put up with him? Why didn't you protect me? He wasn't always so violent, she said. When he came back from his tour, he was never the same. Then he started drinking.

"Well, it is too late now, isn't it?" said Daniel. He was trying not to tear up. Just then Harold walked in.

"Oh, we have a visitor?" said Harold.

"Yes," said Daniel, trying to pull himself together. "This is my mother." Daniel introduced Mr. Brooks.

"Nice to meet you," said his mother.

Harold felt the tension in the room. He excused himself and went out on the porch to smoke his pipe. Daniel changed the subject. "How are you doing?" he asked.

"I'm Ok. Aunt Alice has come to stay for a while. You know you are welcome to come back home."

"Thanks Mom, but I am happy here. The job pays well, and I am saving to go to school."

"Do you still want to be a chef?" she asked. "I miss your cooking."

He smiled. "I will cook dinner for you and Aunt Alice soon."

"That would be very nice." Daniel showed his mother his apartment. Daniel made some tea and offered her some peach cobbler left over from the last evening's supper. When she left, Daniel went to sit on the porch. He watched her drive away.

Harold could see that he was upset. "Are you Ok, Son?" he asked.

After a deep breath and a pause, Daniel said, "'My father died last night."

"Oh, I am sorry to hear that. I thought you had no family."

"I had a family, just not one that wanted me," he said with a wobble in his voice. The two men sat quietly on the porch. After a few minutes, Harold put his arm on Daniel's shoulder. "Family is made out of the people who love you. You know you have family here." Daniel smiled.

Chapter 21
The Truth About Angie

Willow was wandering around the house. Jane had moved to New Hampshire with her mother. They had moved when Jane's father went to prison. Willow was happy for Jane but missed her company. She still had Daniel, but not any female companionship. She wandered into Jonathan's office. Her father was working on some files. She snuggled into a large leather chair near her father's desk. "Dad, why don't you ever speak of Mom?"

Johnathan leaned back in his chair. He knew this was coming someday. He waited a few seconds. Then he sighed. "Because it is painful, and I don't really understand what happened. My life was great for one minute, then the next it was horrible. I had no control over anything. Life just happened to me, and I had to deal with it," said Johnathan."

"I want to know about my mother. Who was she? What was she like? What did you like about her? What did she think about me? I need to know," said Willow, with anguish in her voice.

Johnathan could see that this was serious. "Your mother was a wonderful person. She was the love of my life. She loved you with all her heart."

Willow closed her eyes and was just listening to her father and, watching the events in her head as he was talking about them.

"She used to sing to you, and I would watch her and think that I had everything that I ever wanted. She liked shopping at antique shops."

"Oh, she is wearing a green coat," said Willow. "And she brought a lamp. Do you still have the lamp?" asked Willow.

"No, I gave it to Sofia. She had reddish brown hair. She sang beautifully. She thought I was charming. Can you imagine that? She used to make the best fish and chips. She loved bagel and cream cheese for breakfast. She lit candles every night for supper. She had cold feet that she would stick next to me at night. I loved her then, and I love her still."

Willow was watching the events and smiling. She saw her mother singing to her! Even though it was all in the past, she felt loved. "How did she die?" she asked quietly.

"She fell from the porch while watering the flowers."

Willow started crying uncontrollably.

"No, No, No, Daddy, she was pushed! A man pushed her over the railing. She grabbed onto the flowers, but it didn't help. I can see her falling." Willow was sobbing. "The man dropped something out of his pocket."

"Oh God," gasped Jonathan as he gathered his daughter in his arms with tears in his eyes. He carried her to her room and gently set her on her bed.

"Daddy, tell me more good memories so I can try to forget."

He kissed her head and talked quietly. He tried to fill her head with only nice memories of her mother. "I have something for you," he said. "I will be right back." He came back and laid the green coat over the blankets.

"Oh, it's mom's coat," she said." She stuck her hands in the sleeves with the hood on top of her chest and cuddled into the coat. Jonathan rubbed his hands through his hair, trying to absorb what she said, and waited for her to fall asleep. Then he went downstairs. He opened the secret drawer of Rose Willow's clock that struck 3:32 in the morning. He pulled open the drawer. He checked the contents. There was an abalone hair comb, a bit of change, and a pen. He glanced at the pen. It was engraved, "With love to David."

The Beginning

About The Author

Eugenie is a student of life, wife, mother, woodworker, lover of crafts and cooking, and although short-lived, a pie shop owner. She is Mema to the grandkids, whom she adores and from whom she gets much inspiration. She likes to plant trees, loves life, and tries to be kind.

9 781969 252440